"We'll need all the help we can get on this case," Colton said. "A child's life is involved."

He pulled out onto the highway, the road slick with the fresh snow. "From what I've read about you," he continued, "you've worked on a lot of cases involving children. Why?"

"As a teenager I worked at a day-care center," Lisette said. "At church every Sunday, I took care of the babies. I loved it."

"Then why did you go into law enforcement? Why not a teacher or something?"

"Because I wanted to be like my..." Her voice faltered, and she went quiet.

Colton glanced at her. Her expression was closed, distant, her gaze slanting away from him. He'd hit upon a sensitive subject she didn't want to discuss, which made him only more curious.

* * *

WITNESS PROTECTION: Hiding in plain sight

Safe by the Marshal's Side—Shirlee McCoy, January 2014
The Baby Rescue—Margaret Daley, February 2014
Stolen Memories—Liz Johnson, March 2014
Top Secret Identity—Sharon Dunn, April 2014
Family in Hiding—Valerie Hansen, May 2014
Undercover Marriage—Terri Reed, June 2014

Books by Margaret Daley

Love Inspired Suspense

So Dark the Night
Vanished
Buried Secrets
Don't Look Back
Forsaken Canyon
What Sarah Saw
Poisoned Secrets
Cowboy Protector
Christmas Peril
"Merry Mayhem"
§*Christmas Bodyguard*
Trail of Lies
§*Protecting Her Own*
§*Hidden in the Everglades*
§*Christmas Stalking*
Detection Mission
§*Guarding the Witness*
The Baby Rescue

*The Ladies of Sweetwater Lake
†Fostered by Love
††Helping Hands
   Homeschooling
**A Town Called Hope
   §Guardians, Inc.
‡Caring Canines

Love Inspired

Gold in the Fire
A Mother for Cindy
Light in the Storm
The Cinderella Plan*
When Dreams Come True
Hearts on the Line*
Tidings of Joy
Heart of the Amazon*
†Once Upon a Family*
†Heart of the Family*
†Family Ever After*
A Texas Thanksgiving*
†Second Chance Family*
†Together for the Holidays*
††Love Lessons*
††Heart of a Cowboy*
††A Daughter for Christmas*
**His Holiday Family*
**A Love Rekindled*
**A Mom's New Start*
‡Healing Hearts*
‡Her Holiday Hero*

MARGARET DALEY

feels she has been blessed. She has been married more than thirty years to her husband, Mike, whom she met in college. He is a terrific support and her best friend. They have one son, Shaun. Margaret has been writing for many years and loves to tell a story. When she was a little girl, she would play with her dolls and make up stories about their lives. Now she writes these stories down. She especially enjoys weaving stories about families and how faith in God can sustain a person when things get tough. When she isn't writing, she is fortunate to be a teacher for students with special needs. Margaret has taught for more than twenty years and loves working with her students. She has also been a Special Olympics coach and has participated in many sports with her students.

THE BABY RESCUE
MARGARET DALEY

HARLEQUIN® LOVE INSPIRED® SUSPENSE

Special thanks and acknowledgment to Margaret Daley for her contribution to the Witness Protection miniseries.

Recycling programs
for this product may
not exist in your area.

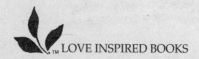 LOVE INSPIRED BOOKS

ISBN-13: 978-0-373-44582-0

THE BABY RESCUE

Copyright © 2014 by Harlequin Books S.A.

www.Harlequin.com

Printed in U.S.A.

For God so loved the world, that he gave his only begotten Son, that whosoever believeth in him should not perish, but have everlasting life.
—*John* 3:16

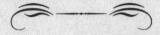

To Marcella,
who has supported me throughout my writing career

ONE

Ice spattered the windshield and laid a thin layer on the streets and sidewalks. Trees began to sag with the extra weight on their limbs. U.S. Deputy Marshal Colton Phillips leaned forward and inspected the roiling dark gray clouds moving in from the west. At least the roads were still passable; the weather lately had been warm in St. Louis, especially for February.

But he didn't have much time to get his witness to the St. Louis Downtown Airport. He was meant to transport the man to his temporary new home in Denver. The pilot of the U.S. Marshals Service's jet had called earlier to warn Colton that, due to the weather, the airport would most likely shut down within forty minutes. Which didn't leave him much time to make the flight.

Colton kept his gaze trained on the lead black SUV in front of his own. He kept some distance between them in case Josh McCall, the marshal driving, had to stop suddenly on the slippery road. Colton had memorized the route to the airport as well as alternative ones in case of trouble. And the more time ticked down and the slower the traffic went, the tenser Colton became.

When they reached a stoplight, he glanced in his rearview mirror at Don Saunders, the low-life criminal who had bargained his way into the Witness Protection Program in exchange for information on a child-smuggling organization. His skin crawled at the sight of Saunders's smug look.

Weasel was too kind of a description for his witness. *Scumbag* fit the man better. Behind Don's cold, small dark eyes, Colton didn't glimpse much intelligence, but what the criminal lacked in that area he made up for with a bulky frame over six and a half feet tall and a rock-hard muscular physique. According to the records, Saunders lifted weights in his spare time between illegal activities—the last being the kidnapping of Annie Duncan and her two-year-old daughter, Sophia.

It wasn't his job to question why a creep like Don Saunders would get into WitSec after what he'd done. But it didn't stop Colton's gut from clenching at the expression on Saunders's face as they slowly wended their way through the traffic toward the airport.

At a four-way stop, Colton waited his turn to proceed, scanning the area. His gaze latched on to the other Denver U.S. Marshal, Quinn Parker, who accompanied him in the backseat next to their witness, his attention glued on Saunders. At least Colton didn't have to worry about the criminal trying to escape while he was driving them. Parker was by-the-book, down to the last detail. His job was to keep Saunders in place while Colton drove or at this moment crept.

The lead SUV crossed the intersection, and Colton pulled up to the corner, his brakes gripping the street but not enough to stop without sliding a few feet.

He looked both ways while Don Saunders mumbled, "You need to go back to driving school."

Colton gritted his teeth and ignored the man's comment—

one of many complaints he'd expounded on in the short time Colton had been in his presence. Deputy U.S. Marshals Josh McCall and Serena Summers had briefed him and Parker on Saunders's activities that led to his being put in WitSec. The man claimed the death of Annie Duncan's husband was just the tip of a huge organization.

An old Mustang approached from the right, slowing down. Colton eased his foot down on the accelerator and started across. The driver of the Mustang suddenly picked up speed, running the stop sign and fishtailing around the corner into the lane ahead of him. Colton slammed on his brakes to avoid hitting the guy. Again Colton lost control for a few seconds as the back end of the SUV swung around partway before coming to a stop. He quickly checked in the rearview mirror behind him, catching sight of Saunders on the right side in back.

With his hands secured behind him, Saunders jerked forward, the seat belt halting his forward motion. The man let out a few choice words. "You're supposed to protect me, not get me killed in a wreck."

"Okay, Parker?" Colton glanced over his shoulder at the other marshal.

"Fine," he muttered, his attention on Saunders, his hand on his gun.

Colton corrected the SUV's direction, then continued forward, falling in behind the Mustang still traveling between him and the lead car. His gut rumbled with tension. He hated it when an operation didn't go exactly as planned. He smiled, thinking back to the perfect operations he had participated in. Not many. That was why he always expected the unexpected.

A white truck trailed their SUV close, only feet from

the bumper. Not good when the streets were icing over. Drivers should know better.

Colton's hands tightened about the steering wheel, the hairs on his nape tingling. Something didn't feel right about this. Nearing another stoplight, he reached for his cell phone to call the lead SUV when the Mustang came to an abrupt halt in front of him, forcing Colton to stomp on the brakes and skid to a stop, missing the car by inches.

The vehicle behind him plowed right into his bumper. The grinding crash of metal on metal filled his ears. The collision jarred his SUV and shoved it into the Mustang. In the side mirror, Colton saw a large man exit the truck and saunter toward him. Colton searched for the lead SUV, which was halfway down the street slowing down, but with the heavy traffic, changing directions wouldn't be easy.

"The guy in the passenger's side is getting out, too. He may have a gun under his coat," Marshal Parker said, pushing Saunders down in the seat.

Wearing a cowboy hat pulled low, the man in the Mustang also jumped out of his car and headed toward the SUV, a thunderous expression carved into his features.

Trapped. A setup?

Colton assessed his chances, made a quick decision and threw his car in Reverse, shoving the truck back a few feet to give him room to maneuver around the Mustang. Then, slamming his car into Drive, he swerved to the left and hit the accelerator as much as he dared with the slick conditions. He left the three men standing in the road. One man stuck his hand in his coat pocket.

"Duck," Colton shouted as he took the corner, tossing a glance in the direction of Josh's car. It had finally made a U-turn and was heading back toward the scene. Colton sped away, not wanting to stick around to find out if a gun was in that man's pocket.

"Everyone okay?" Colton asked as he braked slightly to take another corner ten miles per hour too fast for icy roads. The back of the SUV swerved from one side to the other, but Colton righted it and increased his speed as much as he could afford to.

He glanced at the clock on the dashboard. Twenty-five minutes to get to the plane.

"No, I'm not okay. What if I had been shot? Not to mention the possibility of whiplash. This isn't keeping me safe. If you two can't keep—" Saunders yelled.

"We're fine back here." Parker's calm voice cut into Saunders's tirade.

Keeping his gaze swiveling between the road and his rearview mirror, Colton fumbled for the phone button in the SUV and speed-dialed the other marshals in the lead vehicle. "I'm taking a different route to the bridge. Take care of those guys. I'll get Saunders to the airport," he told Josh McCall.

"I've called for support. A police car isn't far away. When they come, I'll catch up with you."

That might or might not happen. He was on his own as far as Colton was concerned. "Was that little *accident* planned? Do they have guns?"

"Don't know. They're angry and so are the other motorists around them. Traffic is backing up. I'll call you after this is straightened out. How are you going?"

Colton gave Josh another route he'd mapped out in his mind in case something didn't feel right. He always had a backup plan. "If they're after Saunders, how did they know about this transport from the safe house? How did they even know he was in custody?"

"Don't know, but believe me, we'll be looking into it. Keep to the plan. Don't go off doing your own thing." Steel thread ran through Josh's voice—a man whom Colton had butted heads with over how this case should be handled in the short time Colton had been in St. Louis. Since Josh's partner had been killed recently, Colton thought he was afraid to take a risk. It was just as well that Colton's only business there was to transport Saunders to Denver. Actually, Colton had come up with several different ways to get to the airport. Up ahead the stalled traffic forced him to swing his vehicle down a side street and take another direction than what he'd told Josh. Until he knew what was going on, he had to think the worst: those guys in the white truck and Mustang were gunning for Don Saunders.

"This ain't the way you told him." Saunders hugged the door as though trying to get out.

"Worried your boss got wind of your change of allegiance even with all our precautions?" Colton couldn't keep the sarcasm from his voice, glad the specialized lock made it impossible for the man to dive out of the SUV.

"No. Unless you guys told him." Saunders threw a glare at Colton, then Parker.

Saunders was being transported to Denver because one of the pieces of information he told them was that he was supposed to meet a contact there involved in the smuggling ring. He wouldn't say anything else about it until he was out of St. Louis. If anyone got wind of Saunders being in custody, he wouldn't be able to meet the contact in Denver.

Colton took another turn, pushing the SUV as fast as he could safely go if no one suddenly stopped in front of him. "Nope. Kinda hard to tell him anything when we don't know who he is. But remember this deal goes away if you don't keep your end of the bargain."

Saunders snorted. "Please. Quit trying to be the big, tough marshal. I know what's at stake here."

"This big, tough marshal will be in charge of your detail in Denver, responsible for your safety. So play nice."

Parker chuckled. "Yep, you only get to see our pretty mugs for your stay in the Mile High City."

Saunders muttered something under his breath and twisted toward the side window.

Was he watching for the Mustang or white truck? Had he somehow alerted a colleague he was being moved to Denver? Or did the criminals he was going to rat on know he was in the U.S. Marshals' custody? If so, how? His arrest had been kept quiet. As far as the world and Saunders's colleagues knew, he had gotten away from the law enforcement team in the warehouse. But if that accident had been deliberately caused, the ruse might not have worked. Colton checked his surroundings as he weaved his way through the small side streets of St. Louis toward the downtown airport. So far no Mustang or white truck was on his tail. They weren't far away now from their destination, but Colton knew better than to let up on his vigilance. From the times he had worked with Marshal Parker in Denver, he knew Parker was good, but Colton never trusted anyone totally with his life. He'd seen too much to.

As he fell into the flow of the traffic on the Poplar Street Bridge over the Mississippi River, he ground his teeth together. The small jet the U.S. Marshals used to transport witnesses wasn't flying out of the main St. Louis airport, which he prayed would help his chances to get Saunders to the plane without further incident before the big ice and snow storm hit St. Louis full force.

But if someone was watching the four bridges over the river near St. Louis, he could be driving into a trap. No amount of zigzagging through the streets of the city would change the fact that there were ultimately only a few ways to the airport on the Illinois side of the Mississippi. That was if they knew they weren't using the Lambert–St. Louis International Airport.

In the rearview mirror he caught sight of the top of a white truck back five cars. Could it be the same one that had smashed into his SUV? He couldn't take the chance. Pushing his foot down on the accelerator, he changed lanes as he neared the Illinois side of the river.

"We may have a tail," Colton told Parker.

The other marshal pushed Saunders down again, but not without grumbling from the witness. Some people didn't appreciate the efforts the U.S. Marshals Service went through to protect them.

The most direct route to the airport from their position was taking Highway 3. Colton approached the exit. The white truck switched to the same lane. At the last second Colton changed his mind, zipping over the rougher pavement back into the stream of cars to take another exit farther down the road. A few horns honked. He increased his speed, putting as much distance between him and the white truck.

"What are you doing? Are you trying to get us killed?" His face beet red, Saunders straightened to look out the back window.

"Calm down. I know what I'm doing." Colton glimpsed the ashen cast to his partner's face.

"You do?" Saunders asked as Parker again pushed the man down on the seat. "Don't look like it to me. One second you're going off the highway. The next not."

"I took lessons to learn to drive this way."

Saunders harrumphed while Parker laughed, switching his attention between the witness and the traffic behind them. Although glad to have help in keeping an eye on the vehicles around them, Colton didn't drop his own alertness. At least on the east side of the Mississippi River the roads weren't as icy since the cold front just started to blow through the area—possibly giving him enough time to get to the plane before the airport shut down.

Lord, give me the patience to deal with this witness. He's going to test what little I have.

Again Colton proceeded toward an exit, but this time he took it at fifteen miles over the speed limit. He checked his rearview mirror. No white truck. He blew a long breath out slowly. They weren't safe yet. In his mind he pulled up the map he'd studied and began crisscrossing his way toward the west and the airport, coming in a back way.

His car phone rang with a call from Marshal McCall. He punched it on.

"The police rounded up the three guys involved in the accident. They've been taken in for questioning. We don't know if it was intentional or not. They say no, but then that's to be expected. Keep your eyes alert. There could be someone else in case those three failed."

"Assume the worst?"

"You've got it. Are you at the airport yet?" Josh asked.

"Almost. We had to take a detour. I thought I saw the truck behind me on the highway. I guess I didn't."

"Detour? Where? We're on Highway 3 right now, nearing the exit for the airport."

"We're coming in from the other side. Maybe five minutes away. Let them know at the airport." *If all goes well.*

A heavy sigh came through the connection. No doubt Josh McCall wasn't too happy he'd changed the plans without telling him, but Colton had been busy driving in icy conditions.

"See you at the plane." The tightness in the St. Louis–based U.S. Marshal's voice expressed his irritation.

The dark gray clouds raced toward them. Rain splattered the windshield with ice increasingly pelting against the glass. Colton floored the accelerator as much as he dared, only slowing down when he had to make a turn into the airport.

Colton kept his focus on the U.S. Marshals Service's jet parked near a hangar and took the SUV across the fields between runways where the terrain was rough, easier to drive on with ice. He hit a hole in the ground and bounced up, thumping his head on the car's roof. Saunders grunted and spewed a few more curses.

The jet was only another hundred yards away. Once he got Saunders on the plane he could relax, at least until they reached Denver. Then the real work began: getting more useful information from Don Saunders. What they did with it would depend on if those three guys were after Saunders.

Parking near the steps into the jet, Colton threw a glance over his shoulder as he saw the lead SUV heading for them. "Let's get him inside."

He came around to open the back door while Parker moved across the seat and followed Saunders out of the vehicle. As Colton kept watch, Parker hurried their witness onto the jet.

Marshal McCall and his partner, Serena Summers, exited their car and made their way over to Colton. From the body language pouring off the woman whenever she and Josh were together, Colton wondered about how well the pairing of those two marshals was going.

His brown eyes diamond hard, Josh got in Colton's face.

"Your risky driving and going off on your own could have resulted in someone getting killed."

He held his ground and tapped down his anger, saying in a controlled voice, "It didn't and it could have possibly saved our witness's life if that was a planned accident. Sometimes we can't stick around and ask those questions. Our witness is here and safe." With a smile, he nodded toward Serena, a beautiful woman with long brown hair and a look of sadness in her eyes, no doubt from the death of her brother, Daniel, Josh's partner. "Now if you'll excuse me, we need to get out of here while we still can."

As Colton mounted the steps to the jet, his shoulders sagged with weariness, the adrenaline rush subsiding. And this was just the beginning of his part in the case.

FBI Agent Lisette Sutton entered the Supervisory U.S. Marshal Tyler Benson's office in Denver, and two men rose. She supposed the taller one of the pair, standing in front of the oak desk must be U.S. Deputy Marshal Colton Phillips, the person she would be teamed with in this case involving child smuggling and baby brokering across state lines. She shook his hand first, then the marshal's behind the desk.

"I've been assigned to work the Saunders case with you." From growing up in New Orleans, it had taken her years to drop the *y'all* from her speech. Outside of the South, she found that the word didn't sound businesslike— too casual—and she was determined to make it in an occupation still dominated by men.

"Have a seat, Agent Sutton. Your boss called me half an hour ago." U.S. Marshal Benson gestured toward the chair next to her new partner.

As she took the seat, she slid a glance toward U.S. Marshal Phillips, quickly assessing his medium-length dirty-blond hair and strong profile. He swung his gaze toward her and locked on to hers. His startlingly blue eyes fringed in long lashes caught hold of her, and for a moment she couldn't look away. His eyes were intense. Focused. Assessing her as she had him. Her stomach fluttered. Slowly one corner of his mouth tilted up, and he glanced away. Surprised by her momentary reaction to Colton, Lisette centered her full concentration on Benson, resolved not to let anything or anyone divert her from the job to be done.

"From what Don Saunders has given us so far, we're dealing with a black-market baby adoption ring that covers a good part of the United States, possibly even other countries." Benson shuffled a couple of folders until he found the one he wanted and opened it.

That was the reason she would be working with the marshals' team guarding Saunders. If what the man said was true, all kinds of federal laws have been broken. But the reason she'd pleaded with her superior to be assigned to the case was the fact it involved children, her specialty.

Benson cleared his throat. "Now that Saunders is here in Denver and settled into a safe house, we need more. He has additional information he's promised the marshals in St. Louis once he was out of the area. That office went to a great deal of trouble to make it look like Saunders escaped the police so Saunders could maintain his ties with the organization. He insisted on coming to Denver because of some contact he has here. He told them he has a good reason and would tell us when he safely arrives. He has arrived. Time to question the man, and if he's bluffing, call him on it if he wants to remain in WitSec."

"I heard from my boss there was an incident yesterday in St. Louis. What happened? Will that affect his usefulness within the organization?" Shifting toward Colton, Lisette peered at him, wiping any kind of expression from her face. She'd learned to shut down her emotions. She couldn't make a mistake like her mother, a former FBI agent, had. Emotions could get in Lisette's way of doing the best job possible. Her mom had been accused of taking dirty money from a crime scene and then later not backing up her partner. When she'd tried to talk to her mother right after it happened, she wouldn't say much at all, leaving Lisette to think the worst—her mom had betrayed her partner and the FBI.

"A couple of guys interrupted our transport to the airport. I talked with Marshal McCall in St. Louis this morning. They have interrogated the three men involved in the wreck and run background checks. There doesn't appear to be any connection to the criminal elements in St. Louis. The marshals are digging deeper to make sure the trio is exactly what they claim to be. We have to assume at this time they are what they say and proceed forward if we're going to use Saunders's contact in Denver."

"Who are the people involved in the wreck?" Lisette kept her gaze trained on the cleft in Colton's chin, chancing only an occasional glance at his eyes, which were a beautiful sky-blue—attention grabbing. *I never call a man's eyes "attention grabbing." What in the world is going on here?*

Colton zeroed in on her. "The two in the white truck are ranchers who were in St. Louis yesterday on business. The guy in the Mustang works at a hospital and was late for his shift."

"Or so they say. With enough money and expertise a background and identity can be built. You all do it all the time." Lisette lifted her gaze to his, as intense and direct as he was. She could play this game—she could see he was trying to exert his dominance over her early on in their partnership.

"We had him at a safe house in St. Louis—not the U.S. Marshals' office. A limited amount of people knew about him even within the U.S. Marshals Service, so it's not likely he was compromised."

"Could Don Saunders have orchestrated an escape somehow?"

"Again not likely. It's not as if he had access to a phone at the safe house or as if he ever left the place. The only time he made calls was to support the story that he got away. Those calls were monitored."

"Cell phones are small and can be concealed," Lisette said, aware that suddenly it was as if she and Colton were the only two in the office, that his supervisor was a by-stander following their conversation. "If he wasn't kept in a jail cell, he had some freedom at the house. I doubt they had eyes on him twenty-four hours a day."

Colton shifted toward her, his large hands clasping the arms of the chair. "I was one of his guards that last day in St. Louis. He was thoroughly checked for a cell. I've been doing this for years. I know my job." A grin flirted with the corners of his mouth for a few seconds before becoming full-fledged.

"But if he has been compromised in any way, our chance to find out more about this organization and catch the others involved will vanish. A smuggling ring like this can't exist. Children are involved." She hadn't meant for the last sentence to come out so vehemently, but she'd never forget her first case with the FBI—a child abduction that didn't end well. It left a mark on her that she'd never be able to erase, especially since her younger sister had died of SIDS when Lisette was a child. There had been a time she'd wanted a family—children. Now she found that focusing entirely on her career was safer for her emotionally. It was too hard for her to depend on others who could let her down.

Dead seriousness replaced his smile. Colton sat forward, closer to her. "I know exactly what's at stake with this case."

He snared her attention as though trying to read her mind. Silence ruled. Tension charged the air. Her voice had given her away. Had she revealed something else in her expression?

Marshal Benson coughed. "You have a drive ahead of you. Hash it out in the car. We're lead on this case, Agent Sutton, but we value the FBI's input."

In other words, Marshal Colton Phillips would run the show. That didn't mean she wouldn't make her views known. She had six years of experience in the FBI, and before that, she'd been a police officer. "Who is Saunders's contact in Denver? And is this going to help us?" Lisette dragged her gaze from Colton and directed her question to his boss.

Before the man could open his mouth, Colton answered, "That's what we're going to the safe house to find out." He stood. "I'll bring the car around front."

He left his supervisor's office without a backward glance toward Lisette. The atmosphere defused with his departure.

She'd heard Colton was a maverick who often got results by acting and thinking outside the box. She had serious misgivings about working with someone like that. She'd even considered asking her superior to assign another FBI agent when she'd heard who her partner would be. But she couldn't walk away, not when children were involved. That overrode all misgivings she had about her partner for this case. Which left her working with the type of law enforcement officer she tried to steer clear of. Her mother had been like that, doing whatever it took to get the job done, and she'd ended up discredited. She resigned from the FBI not long after Lisette had graduated from the FBI Academy at Quantico. It was not a stellar way to start her career—the daughter of a disgraced agent who hadn't backed up her partner and had been suspected of taking money from a crime scene.

She stiffened her spine. She would make the best of a bad situation and rise above any shortcoming Colton Phillips might have. Then she remembered something else she'd heard about the man: he got results so the U.S. Marshals Service tolerated him.

She wanted to be more than just tolerated. She wanted to prove not all Suttons were the same. She wasn't anything like her mother.

"Agent Sutton, Marshal Phillips is a bit unorthodox, but he does get the job done. After you two get the rest of the information from Saunders, we can then decide the best way to proceed. My children are teenagers, but it wasn't that long ago they were babies. One crime that bothers me more than anything is one against a child. We need to get the people behind this ring."

Lisette rose, gripping the straps of her purse. "I totally agree. If Saunders has any info, we'll get it out of him."

Marshal Benson pushed to his feet and stretched his arm across the desk. "We don't have a lot of time to play with here. According to Saunders, something is going down soon."

Lisette shook his hand. "I understand. Good day."

She took the stairs to the first floor and exited the building, scanning the cars for Colton. A honk sounded in the early morning, drawing her attention. The man climbed from a black Firebird—obviously not a U.S. Marshals Service's vehicle. The highly polished car gleamed in the sunlight.

She approached him. "I'm surprised this Firebird isn't red."

"I thought about that, but I didn't want to be too obvious. I've got to blend into traffic sometimes." He started to round the front. "Let's go."

She watched him. "You want me to drive?"

A look of horror momentarily graced his face, then his expression evened out. "No way anyone else gets behind the wheel of my car." He opened the passenger door. "I was being a gentleman."

A flush seared her cheeks, and she stared at him over the top of the Firebird. "I'll follow you in my car."

"What is it?"

"A navy blue Ford SUV." She gestured toward where it was parked in the lot nearby.

He chuckled. "That screams 'federal agent.' No, we'll use my car."

For a long moment she drilled her gaze into him. He didn't waver but returned her stare. Then she heaved a sigh and skirted the rear to the Firebird. "And your car screams 'I want to drag race.'"

"I haven't tried that. Maybe I'll take up that sport someday."

She slid into the passenger seat, aware of the close interior in the Firebird. She should have insisted on driving them in her SUV, or at the very least following him.

He still held the door. She reached to close it, but he shut it instead. Then he grinned at her and came around to his side, his movements economical and fluid. He caught her staring out the windshield at him and gave her another cocky grin.

She refused to look away.

He settled behind the wheel and started the engine. "I promise you that before this assignment is over, I will show you what this baby can do."

A male and his car. She rolled her eyes and peered out her side window. She'd been excited about the new assignment. It had the potential to prove to her superiors she wasn't anything like her mother, but now she was having major doubts about her partner. This was going to be a *long* assignment.

TWO

Before putting the Firebird into Drive, Colton twisted toward Agent Lisette Sutton. "We need to get a few things straight right from the start." He waited until she turned her head toward him, not one emotion visible on her face. He didn't say anything for a long moment, curious to see what she would do. He hadn't wanted to team up with an FBI agent, especially one he knew nothing about.

One of her eyebrows arched. "We're in a no-parking zone."

"I think it would be safer to talk about this without driving. The conversation needs our full attention."

She released a long breath. "Then tell me before I grow old."

"You and I may not perform our duties the same way, but in this case I am the lead. I just wanted to make sure you heard fully what my boss said about this being under the U.S. Marshals Service's jurisdiction."

"My hearing is perfectly fine." Lisette Sutton fiddled with her glasses.

"Then I have the final say in how we operate. I have been a marshal for ten years with a high success rate. I know what to do."

"I heard you the first time in Marshal Benson's office,"

she said with little inflection in her voice, her expression neutral.

"Good, then there should be no problems between us."

"For your information, I won't blindly follow *anyone's* order." She looked him squarely in the eye, anger piercing through him. "There are rules and procedures in place for a reason."

Colton's gut hardened as though preparing for a punch while his hands balled. "What have you heard about me?"

"I work with an FBI agent who was assigned to Miami at the same time you were. He told me you went into a house without a search warrant, jeopardizing the case."

"But I saved the witness. There wasn't any time to get a warrant. When it comes to people I'm protecting, I do what I must to keep them alive. That is my primary duty." He threw the car into Drive and pulled out into the traffic.

His tight grip around the steering wheel made his hands ache after ten minutes. He loosened his hold. He'd had to grab the witness in the case she'd referred to because of a mess-up with the FBI. The agent for the Bureau had taken an eye off the witness, and he'd escaped because he was scared testifying put him in jeopardy. Colton wondered if she knew the whole story: that the agent responsible had lost his job over the mistake. In Lisette Sutton's point of view Colton had to prove himself, but as far as Colton was concerned, she had to prove herself to him. He trusted no one, and especially not an officer who was inflexible. He'd learned that inflexibility could get a person killed.

The atmosphere in his car could freeze a person faster than a Nor'easter in the dead of winter. Colton kept his gaze trained on his surroundings but occasionally found himself slanting a look toward his partner. Lisette Sutton sat ramrod straight in the passenger seat, her head held high, emphasizing her long, slender neck. Her mouth set in a firm line disguised the fullness of her lips—not that he'd dwelled on that in his supervisor's office or when he'd shared his opinion in the car earlier. But he had to admit her sea green eyes had drawn his attention over and over, even though they were hidden behind those brown-framed glasses she kept fidgeting with. This FBI agent was all business. Her bearing, right down to her blond hair, a deep golden shade, pulled back into a tight bun, shouted that fact to the world. Even her outfit—black pants with a matching suit coat and a plain white blouse—supported that impression.

Maybe, like him, she wasn't too thrilled to be babysitting a criminal like Don Saunders. He understood the need to give deals to catch the big fish in a pond of scum, but it still bothered him when he dealt with ones like Saunders. His faith was the only thing that made this palatable. In the end Saunders would get his due. He would be held accountable for his actions with the Lord.

"How much farther is it?" Lisette Sutton asked in a husky voice that almost betrayed her businesslike demeanor.

"Another fifteen minutes. The safe house is out a ways—not a lot of neighbors to wonder what's going on."

"Also harder for Mr. Saunders to catch a ride somewhere."

"True."

"Who's with him right now?" She shifted toward him, her posture not as tense as before.

And for some reason that made the confines of his car even smaller. His gut clenched at the same time his hands did on the steering wheel. "Marshals Janice Wallace and

Neil Simms. The other on the team is Quinn Parker, who will be at the house later."

He took the exit off Interstate 70. At the intersection of the off ramp and a country road, he came to a stop and made the mistake of glancing at her. His gaze collided with hers. A faint red colored her cheeks, and she turned away.

Her stiff carriage returned, her shoulders thrust back. The temperature in the car dropped even more. He made a right turn onto the two-lane highway, a wall of mountains on his left blanketed with snow. At least the roads were cleared.

"Is our destination up in the mountains?" She finally broke the silence a few miles down the road.

"No, at the foot of one. The area around here is beautiful and worth exploring in your free time. Have you had a chance to do much sightseeing?"

"No."

"How long have you been in Denver?"

"Six months. How about you?"

"Two years." About the extent he would stay in any one place. That was why he had applied for the open position in St. Louis. Colton was bummed that he didn't get it. "How do you like Denver so far? Have you found a place to stay yet?" he asked, trying to play nice with the Ice Queen and learn about his new partner.

"When I first moved here, I lived in one of those extended-stay hotels. Hated it. I was out searching for a place every spare moment I had. I found a nice acceptable apartment in only a week."

"I still haven't gotten around to finding an apartment. I don't mind the extended-stay hotel I'm at. It's just a place to sleep. I'm looking to move to another assignment when this case is over with." Why did he reveal that? He didn't usually offer much personal information even to someone he was working with.

"During that week I felt like I lived out of my suitcase. Hotels always give me such a temporary feeling."

He shrugged. "I'm used to that. It doesn't bother me. No obligation on my part. No lease." There was a time it had bothered him. But as a child, after his third move to yet another foster home, he'd begun to accept that would be his normalcy, and he'd better get used to it. So everywhere he lived he'd learned to accept it was only temporary, and eventually he embraced that way of life. Even as an adult he moved a lot, usually only staying at a post no more than a year or two. It was easier that way. He didn't become invested in his coworkers' lives. So much better when he left if he wasn't too close to his coworkers.

Colton turned onto a gravel road still covered with snow that winded through some tall pines and aspens. He called the marshals in the cabin where Saunders was being kept. "I'm nearly there. I'm glad to see no fog." He gave his team members the code with the last sentence to let them know that he hadn't been compromised. "Is everything all right?"

"Just peachy. Nothing unusual has happened," Marshal Janice Wallace said, her voice getting lower with each word. "Except this witness is driving me crazy. Otherwise, Neil and I are having a grand ole time."

"The cavalry is here to rescue you two." He peered through the trees as he approached a bend in the road. "In fact, I'm pulling up now." He took the curve, coming upon a log cabin in a small clearing with various evergreens mixed in with deciduous trees surrounding the open space. A blanket of pristine snow stretched out from the safe house.

"Yeah, we saw you coming and cheered. I'm surprised

you didn't hear us from the main highway," Marshal Wallace said in reference to the two hidden cameras posted at the beginning of the gravel road.

"Was that the noise I heard? Glad you cleared that up." Chuckling, Colton disconnected.

"Did something happen?" Agent Sutton—no, at least in his thoughts she was Lisette—panned the area as she unbuckled her seat belt.

"No, other than Saunders. He has such a winning personality that it doesn't take long for him to drive a person crazy with his complaints and whining. When we had that incident on the way to the airport in St. Louis, he griped the whole way that I was trying to kill him. Believe me, if I had wanted to, he would be dead now."

Lisette's intriguing green eyes widened.

He grinned. "Just kidding."

She blinked and pushed the door open, her professional facade completely in place. "I know that." Her hand went to her glasses to straighten them.

He made her nervous. That was her sign—adjusting her glasses.

Marshal Wallace swung the door open and stood in the entrance. The tall woman with short black hair smiled. "Nice to see you two. Come in." She stepped to the side, introducing herself to Lisette as they shook hands.

Colton entered the cabin behind Lisette, who paused a few feet inside to scan the large room with a massive fireplace along the back wall, a kitchenette off to the right and a hallway that led to the single bedroom. He liked the defensible layout. There was only one way into the cabin with one window in the bedroom; there were none in the bathroom or kitchen and three in the living area. Off to the side he noticed the computer sitting with shots of various camera views of the terrain and road near the safe house.

"Where's Saunders?"

Marshal Neil Simms swiveled around in the chair before the laptop. "Hi, I'm Neil, Lisette." He smiled, then turned his attention to Colton. "Still sleeping. He was up late complaining of his digs. You should wake him, or he'll be up late again tonight when Janice and I have to take over."

"But he no doubt needs his beauty sleep. The trip here yesterday was a tiring, stressful one." Colton pressed his lips together to keep from grinning.

The two marshals on the night shift started for the exit. "Quinn is on his way here," Simms said, and then opened the front door. "We'll be back this evening. Have fun."

The echo of the door clicking shut filled the small cabin. Colton looked at Lisette, who prowled the perimeter, glancing out each window. "I'm surprised those two didn't wake up Saunders right before we showed up." He strode toward the hallway to check on their witness.

"You're going to wake him?" Amusement laced Lisette's voice.

"You know the adage about never waking up a sleeping baby? I think it applies in this case, too, but I want to check on him."

Her light laughter drifted to him as he made his way down the short hallway, checking the bathroom before opening the door to the bedroom. Saunders stood at the small window peering out.

"If you're thinking of escaping, I'm not sure you would fit through it. In fact, I know you wouldn't."

Saunders stiffened his shoulders and pivoted toward Colton. "I thought I was rid of you, that they would fire you for your incompetence yesterday."

"That incompetence is what would have saved you if those guys had been assassins. You could be dead if I had waited around to chitchat with them."

"How do you know they weren't sent to kill me?"

"Because we set up your cover well and those guys are being checked out thoroughly. We won't proceed if they don't check out."

"Then how in the world do I know if I'm safe here?" Saunders pursed his mouth, thinning his cheeks.

"Unless you called someone, no one knows you're in Denver." Out of the corner of his eyes, Colton spied Lisette coming down the hall.

"You do. And the other two marshals guarding me last night." Saunders's eyes flared. "And her."

Colton gritted his teeth. *Lord, where is that patience?*

Lisette positioned herself to his left and slightly behind him. "Mr. Saunders, I'm from the FBI and here to ask you some questions. Please come into the living room." Her voice held a hint of a Southern accent, warm and almost inviting, adding a certain charm to her words.

Saunders stared at her for a long moment. "At least this lady is nice to look at. Can't say that about the other one."

Tension whipped down Lisette's length and flowed from her in waves. "I beg your pardon." The glare she sent Saunders would put most people who were smart in their place.

But not their witness. He roared with laughter. "Sassy, too. I bet you're a handful."

"In the living room, Mr. Saunders," she said in a tight, husky voice, her Southern drawl more pronounced, but nothing warm and inviting in the tone anymore.

Interesting. The more angry Lisette Sutton became, the more her Southern heritage came out. Colton let Saunders move into the hall where the man faced Lisette.

"What are you afraid of? That some man might think you're pretty if you let your hair down, took off those ridiculous glasses and wore proper feminine clothes?"

Lisette drilled her sharp gaze into Saunders to the point he frowned and continued his trek into the living area without another word.

"Are you okay?" Colton almost felt indignant for her at the sneer in Saunders's voice.

She lifted her chin. "Of course. I won't let someone like him get to me." She adjusted her brown-framed glasses and followed Saunders.

"I heard that, little missy," Saunders said with a laugh.

She didn't break stride but kept going into the main room. Colton trailed her, admiring how she walked—like a soldier going into battle.

Silently he applauded her bravado. He'd read she was a good interrogator; this was one of the reasons she was assigned to this case. Saunders had been playing games with the U.S. Marshals Service from the first moment he was arrested in the warehouse and told them he had information that could lead to the downfall of a large child-smuggling network. He either had to produce useful information, or he would go to jail per the agreement Saunders had signed. Colton hoped Lisette could draw the information out of him.

Lisette sat at the kitchen table that seated four and gestured for Saunders to take the chair across from her. Colton decided to stand back and assess the witness while she started the interview.

She opened the folder she'd brought concerning the case, her movements precise, deliberate. "I see here you claimed that Joe Delacorte's death was the tip of the iceberg, as per your conversation with Marshals McCall and

Summers, who talked with you last in St. Louis. So what are you implying?"

"Can't you read?" Saunders flipped his hand at the folder. "It should be in there."

"What was Delacorte messed up in?"

He came up from the chair and leaned across the table. "As I told the marshals in St. Louis, child smuggling from all over."

"Please sit down," she said in a calm, soft voice. "This can be an easy process or a long and difficult one that sends you to prison in the full population. You know how some criminals feel about crimes involving babies. It doesn't sit well with them. There is no telling what could happen to you in jail, not to mention if your boss found out you had been talking to us to cut a deal."

Saunders snorted but sank back in his chair.

Colton lounged against the kitchen counter to watch the match. She was good. His respect went up a notch. She glanced toward Colton, giving the witness time to think over what she had said. In the instant their gazes met, a connection linked them, more than this case. It held for a few seconds before she severed it and swung her attention back to Saunders.

Confused, Colton pondered his reaction to their shared look and nearly missed her next question.

"What were the plans for Sophia Duncan? Why was she singled out? And then what about the other children? Do they all end up in St. Louis? You said you had specific information to share with us." She shut the file, crossed her arms and set them on top of the folder.

Colton forced himself to focus on Saunders. He didn't need to be distracted by his temporary partner.

Saunders shrugged. "Don't know about all the kids. I

know from my brother Luke he took jobs in Kansas, Illinois and Iowa and those came to St. Louis."

"But you don't know about other states or where those babies ended up?"

"No, except Colorado. That's why we're here."

"When your brother was arrested for the murder of Delacorte, did you take over for him in the organization?"

"Take over?" Saunders's mouth twisted.

"Yes, your hearing is good. Did you take your brother's place?"

Saunders looked at Colton. "I have full immunity with anything involving this case?"

"Only if you fulfill the agreement you made with the government prosecutor."

The lowlife took a deep breath and expelled it slowly. "Yes, Luke and me worked together. My next job was to pick up a package here in Denver and wait for instruction where to take it."

So this was the reason Saunders wanted to be here in Denver. Was the package he was picking up a baby? Or information about the organization? Colton pushed off the counter and approached the man, hovering over him. "It? What are you picking up?"

Disdain flittered across Saunders's face. "A baby, of course. Haven't you been listening?"

"When?"

"I don't know."

"From who?"

"I don't know."

Colton got down in his face. "What *do* you know?"

Lisette relaxed back in her chair, enjoying the exchange between the two men. One thing the FBI agent from Miami had said about Colton Phillips was that he was a good interrogator, usually getting what he wanted from his witness.

Saunders smirked. "What's this? Bad cop, badder cop?"

Colton pulled back and crossed his arms over his chest, his expression chilling, the blue of his eyes arctic cold. "This isn't working. I'll be reporting to my supervisor that you haven't given us any useful information, which means you're in violation of your agreement with the government."

Saunders's sneer fell. He blinked rapidly and turned his regard to Lisette, as if she would rescue him. Fixing a stare on him, she wanted him to squirm for a little bit. "We aren't going to keep spending thousands of dollars to keep you safe if you aren't going to fulfill your part of the bargain. Would you, if you were in our shoes?"

Saunders's cackles resonated through the cabin. "Never in a thousand years would I be a cop."

"We know this is about child smuggling. Tell us something we don't know. Who is your boss in St. Louis?"

"I don't know his name. All I have is a burner phone I use to get my instructions, which you have now."

"Then what use are you to us? Marshal Phillips, make your call to your supervisor. This is a dead end." She narrowed her eyes, boring into the man across from her. Silence fell. Colton towered over the witness but didn't say a word.

"Okay. Okay. Right before I was apprehended, this was all set up. I'm supposed to meet my contact in a few days at a masquerade ball for charity. If I check out, then he'll give me the information where to pick up the baby."

"Where are you supposed to take the baby once you have it?"

"My boss will call me with instructions once the hand-off is successful." He looked back and forth between Colton and Lisette. "You have my burner phone. Maybe that can help you."

She bent forward. "You know it doesn't help. Is this all you have? Where's the information about who might be behind this baby-smuggling ring that you insinuated you had in St. Louis?"

"I—I can't…"

"You can't or you won't?" She raised her voice.

Saunders snapped his mouth closed and pinched his lips together.

Colton kicked the legs of the table nearest Saunders. "That's it. The deal is off. You're going back to St. Louis. You've been playing us for fools."

THREE

"You can't do that!" Saunders shot to his feet, color draining from his face. "You promised to protect me. I'm putting my life on the line because of you."

"Mr. Saunders, please take a seat." Lisette forced a calmness into her voice while she worked to keep her emotions—anger, frustration, impatience—from showing in her expression. "Marshal Phillips has been dealing with you longer than I have and is no doubt tired of these games you're playing. Give me a reason not to go along with him." The stab of Colton's razor-sharp look sliced through her, but she ignored him. However, his warning that he was in charge kept blaring in her mind.

Saunders eased back into his chair, drawing in a deep breath. "I can't tell you who the bosses of the smuggling ring are because I don't know who they are, but I do know there are several running it. A person only knows who they directly work for. I've worked with a middleman for this part of the country a lot lately. I'm supposed to get the baby and deliver it to him. So until I meet my contact at the party and find out where to pick up the baby, I can't tell you who the middleman is." He paused, probably for dramatic effect, then continued, "Except he goes by Jackson. I don't know if that's a first or last name. We've been working together for over a year so I'll have to be there. In fact, I have to call him the day of the party to make sure everything is still set up."

Lisette frowned. "So this Jackson is the middleman?"

"He has a lot more knowledge about the operation than I do. I deliver the babies, and he takes over from there. I don't know what he does with them after that."

"How are you going to make contact with the courier at the party? I imagine there will be hundreds in attendance." Colton leaned back against the counter again. "It's a big charity event for children." Her partner choked out the last word, a frown descending on his face.

Lisette didn't blame him. The irony of this whole situation struck her.

"I'm not to wear a mask. He'll recognize me and approach me. Jackson has given the contact a picture of me."

"How interesting—you have made yourself indispensable if we want to catch a higher-up in the ring." Sarcasm dripped from Colton's voice.

While Lisette felt the same as Colton, her brief look conveying that to the marshal, she had to be the "good" cop in this scenario. "So you'll be turning over this middleman you report to in exchange for the deal?"

Saunders nodded. "And don't forget the baby who won't become part of the smuggling operation. You didn't really know what was going on until I decided to talk in St. Louis. All that has to be worth something. Even the fact that the organization has several levels. I'm at the bottom of the rung. It's a start you didn't have before me."

Colton pulled back the chair and sat between her and Saunders at the kitchen table. "Tell you what. We'll go along for the time being. But if you don't deliver at least the middleman and the baby, then the bargain is off."

Lisette wasn't sure Colton had that kind of authority, but by his no-nonsense tone and fierce, determined stare, it would be foolish on Saunders's part not to snatch up the deal.

"Sure. Sure. You'll be the hero getting this information. Jackson has dealings with the higher-ups." Saunders put his hands on the top of the table and began to push up, saying, "Well, if you two don't need me, I'm taking a nap."

Colton clasped Saunders's lower arm. "Don't play me. You don't want to rile me." His look emphasized the threat behind his words.

Saunders peered at Colton as though trying to gauge his intent and then grinned. "I hear you. I'm no fool. I know that I have no other choice."

Colton released his grasp, and Saunders scurried toward the bedroom like the rat he was.

"You're positive he can't fit through the window?" Lisette asked when their witness disappeared from view.

"Yes. But even if he tried, when he opened the window, an alarm would go off. We'd know and go outside and wait for him to become stuck."

"At least we'll know where he is at all times."

He chuckled "Might be a bit chilly, especially at night, and then there are the bears that might be curious."

"I thought they hibernated in the winter."

"They have been sighted from time to time."

"What do you know about Don Saunders?"

"I'd think of him like I would a rattlesnake. Deadly. He'll make a lot of racket to ward us off, but when push comes to shove, he'll strike without a second thought to save himself."

"I have a feeling you don't trust easily." Lisette rose,

needing to pace—do something. This wasn't the part of the job she liked—sitting around and waiting.

"No. People usually end up disappointing me. But then I guess that goes with the line of work we're in. How about you?"

"I have to agree with you. I've been burned, which makes me hesitate to trust others." Especially when the people in question were her mother and a fellow FBI agent she thought she was in love with until the drama concerning her mom made Lisette a pariah within the Bureau.

"You know, I should have taken exception to what you said to Saunders, that you wanted a reason not to go along with me. What part of our conversation in the car did you need me to go over? The part where I'm the lead on this team?"

She moved toward the window that afforded a view out the front of the cabin. The other two windows in the living room flanked the fireplace and looked out the back. "I thought I would be the good cop and get him to think I was on his side." She swept around to face him, only a few feet from her. When had he moved? Why hadn't she heard him? As he continued toward her, her throat went dry. "It worked. If he can deliver what he says, it'll get us closer to who is behind this smuggling ring."

He paused an arm's length away. "There is more than one person at the top. That's the first I heard of that. He didn't say anything about that to the St. Louis marshals."

"See what happens when he's rattled." Lisette thought of moving back, giving herself some space, except that the window was there. The dryness spread from her throat to her mouth. Energy pulsated from Colton, reaching out and wrapping around Lisette. She sidestepped and put some distance between them.

"That's why I did what I did. I never do something without a reason."

"So you aren't impulsive?"

"Being impulsive can get you killed. You have to be constantly thinking ahead and making plans how to act or react. You always have to have a backup plan or two."

"Is that what happened on the way to the airport yesterday?"

He nodded. His gleaming eyes fixed on her, and he quirked a grin. "We did make a good team with Saunders."

The word *team* resounded through her thoughts. From what she'd read about Colton, he wasn't exactly a team player. She hoped he didn't blow this case. She needed to make a good impression with her new boss. Denver was the first time she'd been assigned to a larger office. For six years she'd been relegated to some of the worst assignments in the FBI, even though she'd been one of the top in her class at the FBI Academy. No one had said anything, but she knew it was because her mother had to resign from the Bureau. Lisette would have to work twice as hard as others to prove her worth as an agent.

She pinned him with her regard. "Communication is the key to a good team." *Remember that before you mess up my chance at a better job in the FBI.*

Colton finished his walk-through at the hotel where the charity masquerade ball was being held. The place was as secured as it could be with three hundred guests attending the party. Not a bad choice for a rendezvous to pass along information in an illegal activity. Most guests would be masked and the ballroom filled to capacity. It would be easy for Saunders to get lost in the crowd and slip away unnoticed if he and his team weren't vigilant.

Marshal Quinn Parker approached, dressed in a joker costume. "Who in the world picked out this for me to wear?" He waved his hand down his length.

"You can blame it on Melissa. Is there a reason she would choose you to wear the joker outfit?" Colton imagined his boss's secretary having a good laugh over what she picked out for them.

Parker laughed. "Have you looked at yourself lately? The only time I see a man wear tights is at a ballet."

"You go to the ballet?"

Parker narrowed his eyes. "My wife drags me. Who are you supposed to be?"

Colton donned his velvet hat like the ones worn in the fifteenth century and bowed at the waist. "Romeo, at your service."

"Where's your Juliet?"

Colton looked behind Parker at the woman coming toward them. Lisette wore a dress that would be from the same time period as his costume. She moved gracefully in a long crimson gown with an elaborate beaded and jeweled bodice cut with a square neckline. Although what she had on was elegant, what caught Colton's attention was Lisette's long flowing golden curls hanging below her shoulders, and her eyes, accented with shades of brown eye shadow, no longer hidden behind glasses. So she did have contacts. Interesting. Why did she feel the need to hide her beauty? There was no doubt she was gorgeous.

"Ah, your Juliet has arrived. I wonder what Benson's secretary had in mind doing that," Parker said when he glanced at Lisette.

No doubt she was messing with Colton's mind. His supervisor's secretary loved to play practical jokes. He was the target this time. "Since I've been forced to wear tights,

I need some kind of compensation." Colton covered the few feet to Lisette and bowed with a flourish. "I like your hair down. You should wear it like that more often."

Lisette pursed her lips. "We have worked together three days, and you profess to know how I usually wear my hair?"

He winked at her. "Yep. The way I've seen you the past few days is the way you go to work all the time."

"Unless I'm undercover."

"How often has that happened?"

"This is the first time."

"In other words, you never wear your hair down."

"Yes, I do. On my days off."

He stepped closer and lowered his voice. "What do you like to do on your days off?"

"Wear my hair down. Be myself."

He wondered what that was. "Without your glasses?"

"Sometimes. What does this have to do with tonight's assignment?"

Two pink patches on her cheeks held his attention until he realized he was staring. He cleared his throat and said, "I wanted to make sure you could see clearly in case something went wrong?"

One of her eyebrows rose. "Are you sure that's the reason?"

How in the world had he let this conversation become personal? He was the team leader. He had to consider everything, didn't he? He shifted his gaze toward Parker. "Saunders is ten minutes out. Marshals Simms and Wallace are bringing him to the party."

"Oh, joy. His appearance is going to ruin a perfectly nice evening." She sauntered past him and greeted Parker.

For a brief moment Colton pictured himself with Lisette, attending this charity ball as a couple on a date. Not having to work. Not having a witness to protect. Having dinner beforehand. Sharing a dance—

"Marshal Phillips," Lisette broke into his daydream, "Parker is going to recheck the west corridor and exit. I'm taking the east."

He shook away the mental image of her clasped in his arms. "I'll see about the north. Simms and Wallace are bringing him in through the south entrance. Meet me back here in five minutes so we can cover the south as Saunders arrives."

Colton hurried toward the north hallway, a vision of Lisette teasing the edges of his mind, trying to work its way back into his thoughts and rob him of his concentration on the job. All because she wore her hair down! His fingers itched to run through her thick blond curls. He never got involved with a coworker. It was not a good idea, especially with the job he had. So why now was he attracted to her?

He waved at an extra marshal brought in to be posted at the north door. Brad Worth nodded at him, then returned his focus to the entrance. After Colton checked a few rooms off the hallway to make sure they were still locked, he started back the way he came.

When he'd been in foster care, he'd learned not to become too attached to anything or anyone. His job had only reinforced that—traveling a lot and moving from one U.S. Marshals' office to another. Yes, those moves had been his choice because he was used to being in places temporarily. What would happen if he stayed put for more than two years in a town?

As Colton neared the south entrance, he tamped down all feelings. This was business tonight. He'd done this enough times to run on autopilot. Agent Lisette Sutton was a professional, and that was all it was. He admired that in any law enforcement officer.

Through her earpiece Lisette could hear the conversation between Saunders, dressed in a pirate's costume, and a woman in a Little Bo Peep outfit standing near the long dessert table. Lisette had verified everyone was in position for the exchange that should happen soon between Saunders and his contact, and now she moved across the dance floor to Colton. She grimaced. The annoying man who had driven everyone crazy the past few days was poised close by.

"Would you like to dance?" Saunders asked the lady dressed as Little Bo Peep minus the staff.

"I'd love to," came the faint answer to his question.

Lisette paused next to Colton, facing the dance area as the slow song started. "I wonder if our guy can waltz."

"We're about to find out."

She followed Saunders and Little Bo Peep as he swept his partner out onto the floor with the other pairs. "Nope. He doesn't have a clue how to waltz. Probably doesn't even realize it is one."

"In his line of work, I doubt he has a need to."

"I guess in ours we don't, either."

"No, but for some it's a pastime."

She slid a look toward him for a few seconds before returning it to Saunders. "Ballroom dancing?"

A smile curled the corners of his mouth. "Yeah, one of the marshals I worked with went out dancing every weekend he could with his girlfriend. Later they got married and they still do it. He told me it's his exercise."

"I never thought about that."

"Do you dance?"

"Not much." She didn't date a lot, not after her boyfriend in the FBI dropped her because of the scandal involving her mother. Building her career was her life, and finally after years she felt it was beginning to pay off. With the assignment to the Denver office, she felt the FBI was satisfied she wouldn't turn out like her mother had, which meant Lisette would work extra hard to keep that impression true. This case with the U.S. Marshals Service was a big break for her.

"Then how did you know it was a waltz?"

"I love music—all kinds. I also love to watch people dance."

"But you don't?"

She could feel his eyes on her. "Not much chance. It takes two."

"I see Saunders is moving out of our range. Should we?" Colton held out his hand to her.

"You can waltz?"

"I'm a quick study, and I saw my colleague and his wife do it enough. At least I'll be better than Saunders."

Lisette placed her hand in his, the contact sending a tingling sensation zipping up her arm. He grasped her at the waist, and she nearly stepped on his foot when she tripped over her own. Warmth suffused her face. "Sorry. I didn't have a friend to show me."

Lisette listened to the soft rhythm of the song and fell into sync with Colton. He moved them toward Saunders. All Lisette heard through her earpiece were the music and the background din of the crowd in the ballroom. Saunders was quiet.

Halfway across the dance area from Saunders, Colton swept her around and she faced Saunders.

Saunders swung his partner around and crashed into a waiter.

"Watch where you're going, dude." The waiter's loud words blared through her earpiece.

"Sorry. Got carried away."

The man who had collided with Saunders strode away from him and his partner. Saunders moved toward the far end of the dance floor in a couple of twirls as though he had all of a sudden learned to waltz.

"I think he just made contact with that waiter who collided with him," she said close to Colton's ear as the song came to an end.

He swung her around to look at Saunders. "He's just disappeared in the swarm leaving the floor." He dipped his head and spoke into his mike in a soft voice. "Find Saunders, south end of the ballroom. Agent Sutton thinks he made contact and is now lost in the crowd."

Lisette was headed in the direction where she'd last seen Saunders when suddenly the lights went out. Darkness descended over the ballroom, leaving only the muted light of the red exit signs.

FOUR

All around Colton, lights from people's cell phones illuminated the ballroom, the soft glow enough to see where a person was going. Using his, he closed the short space between him and Lisette while saying to the team, "Cover the exits. We can't let Saunders escape."

"The rest of the hotel is lit. The blackout only affected this wing," Quinn Parker came back on the comlink.

"Thankfully the team members are dressed as hotel security in case this isn't related to Saunders. I'll cover the left side of the ballroom, and when I get my hands on him, it might not be pretty," Lisette whispered, then took off her mask.

Chuckling, he removed his, too, so nothing obscured his view. "He's a valuable asset. We can't treat him like a criminal. Meet me at the main door."

Over a PA system a hotel employee made an announcement there was a technical problem that affected this part of the hotel. "We're working on getting the lights back on. Please exit the ballroom in an orderly matter."

Colton turned to the right and began searching for Saunders among the guests making their way toward the exits. This was a time he was glad for the convenience of cell phones and the flashlight app a person could download. No one was panicking in the dark.

His team members called in one by one to let him know they were in place, watching the guests as they filed out of the ballroom. While Colton weaved his way toward the back, scanning faces, he kept listening to his earpiece for any sounds from Saunders. All he heard were voices talking about the lights going out. The man must be in the crowd—somewhere.

Once he secured him again, he would get to the bottom of why the lights went out. About ten feet from him on the left, a large man built like Saunders, dressed in black, had his back to Colton. He pushed his way through the throng toward the person. When he got a better view, his shoulders relaxed. The man wasn't in a pirate costume.

"How's it coming getting these lights on?" Colton spoke into his comlink.

"It shouldn't be long," Janice said. "The good news is I don't think Saunders could have done it. At least not personally. The control box isn't near."

He didn't trust Saunders one bit, but the deal the government had made with the criminal was a good one. Could someone in Saunders's organization know about Saunders being in WitSec and recognized he was being watched?

"Where are you guys?" blasted through Colton's earpiece.

He didn't have a means to answer Saunders as the man only wore a listening device. But Colton wanted to shout, "Tell us where you are." From what he'd read about Saunders and seen over the past few days, the man's intelligence wasn't in the genius level.

"I can't find anyone in this mess," the annoying voice whined.

"Lisette, you hearing this?" Moving, Colton panned the faces of the people around him.

"Yes, but I'm almost to the back and I haven't seen him."

"Maybe he'll make it to an exit. They're all covered, so he can't get out without being spotted."

A few curse words came through Colton's earpiece, and he wanted to yank it out. But he didn't.

"Quit stepping on my toes," Saunders yelled.

Suddenly a couple of yards to the right, the crowd pushed back. Shouts and sounds of fists hitting flesh came through the earpiece. Colton rushed toward the commotion, shoving his way through the people fleeing away. A ring of spectators circled two men fighting—one Saunders.

"Found him," Colton said into his comlink, then dove into the melee, straight for Saunders, who had pinned a man to the floor and continued to pummel him. Colton grabbed Saunders's arm and jerked him upright. "Lisette, I need help in the northeast corner of the ballroom. Everyone else stay where you are."

The guy on the floor scrambled to his feet, swiping his hand across his face to wipe the blood away, smearing his white clown paint. "You're going to pay for this." He balled his hands and charged Colton, standing between him and Saunders. Colton backed away, but the enraged guest barreled into him. "You can't protect him. He started it."

Colton held the clown by the shoulders, getting into his face, while the angry combatant tried to skirt around Colton to get at Saunders.

"You stepped on my foot," Saunders shouted behind Colton. "You might have broken my toe."

"I did not. It was an accident." The man's breath reeked of alcohol. His face reddened where the white paint was gone. Colton suspected his blood pressure was sky-high.

Lisette parted the crowd and appeared at Colton's side. He glanced sideways and mouthed the words, "Help me."

She edged even closer, wedging her way between him and the man he held. "Can I help you? You're bleeding." Lifting a cloth napkin toward his face, Lisette smiled at the injured clown. "Come with me. I'll take care of you." Her voice held a lilting Southern drawl.

Colton pivoted toward his charge and gripped his arm, tugging him toward the wall. "What were you thinking, calling attention to yourself?"

"Protecting myself. Where were you?" Saunders glared at him. "I'm probably gonna have a black eye from his punch."

Colton had no compassion for Saunders. He made alienating others an art form. "I have a feeling the man you were hitting will have more than that." Dragging a chair to his witness, he continued, "Sit and don't move." Standing next to Saunders, Colton searched the area to see where Lisette went with the other guy.

"This isn't as bad as I thought it would be." Lisette dipped the end of the napkin in a glass of water and dabbed it against the clown's face, painted white except around his nostrils. "You lost your nose."

"That was the first thing to go," the man grumbled. "I ought to sue him."

"For a missing clown nose?" Lisette grinned while slanting a look toward Colton and Saunders. She continued wiping at the clown's white makeup, trying to get a better picture of the man.

"I'm going to owe the costume shop for it." He clasped her hand. "I'm going to the bathroom and take care of the rest of this mess. Thanks for your help."

She gave him the wet napkin, then reached up to his red wig. "It's askew. Let me fix it?"

"Lady, it's fine." He drew back; his dark eyes, outlined in black and red paint, widened. "I'm fine." Then he stomped off in those big shoes he wore.

The lights came on in the ballroom, revealing half of the attendees gone and the other half still trying to leave. Lisette glanced around her, seeing Quinn at the door nearest her. She nodded at him, then strode to Colton and Saunders. "Tell me the hand-off went down."

"Of course. When the lights went out, I got turned around. I don't have no cell phone like the others." Saunders rose. "Looks like the party is over an hour early."

Colton scanned the area around them. "It is for us. We're leaving. Make your way to the far right door, then keep walking back the way you came into the hotel."

One of Saunders's bushy eyebrows lifted. "Alone?"

"Oh, you'll never be alone. We'll be there."

As Saunders strolled toward the exit, Colton put his arm around Lisette. His touch surprised her.

"In case anyone is watching. We're a couple concerned by the fight." He began leisurely sauntering in the same direction as Saunders. "What did you think about the clown? Did you find out anything about who he is?"

"No, in fact, when I started wiping his face, he took over and said he would take care of it in the restroom."

"Wouldn't hurt to check the one nearest the ballroom. Maybe I can get a better glimpse of him."

"Do you suspect him of something?"

"I suspect everyone in this room."

"Even me?" Lisette tried to tamp down the feelings he generated by his close proximity. She wasn't succeeding.

Her heartbeat increased, and for a few seconds she had a hard time focusing on the mission at hand.

"Should I?"

"The U.S. Marshals Service approached the FBI, not the other way around."

"Then I don't," he said with a laugh.

She wanted to punch him in the arm.

At the exit he stepped away from the people still leaving the ballroom and turned his back to them, then a minute later he returned. "I let the team know we would be along after I check the men's restroom. Quinn said a disheveled clown rushed out the door he was guarding and disappeared in the crowd heading toward the north entrance to the hotel. There's a restroom near there."

While Colton ducked inside the bathroom, Lisette stood guard, watching everyone passing her. What happened to the woman Saunders was dancing with when the lights went out? She remembered what she looked like. The lady dressed as Little Bo Peep wore a thin black mask that didn't conceal her face as much as some of the others in the ballroom.

When Colton returned from the bathroom, he shook his head, a frown marring his features.

"Maybe he went home instead."

"Yeah, maybe. But there were five minutes Saunders was out of sight. A lot can happen in five minutes." Colton slipped his arm around her waist and started for the south entrance.

"But he didn't try to escape."

"True. But we're going to get the surveillance camera footage from the hotel and see about identifying the people who attended."

"Three hundred? What do you think happened?"

"I don't trust Saunders. I want to cover everything in case something goes wrong later. Too many things happened tonight to be pure coincidence."

"And we should look more closely at who the waiter, the clown and Little Bo Peep were. See if we can identify them. They had physical contact with Saunders toward the end."

"First we need to get him back to the cabin safely. We'll follow Janice and Neil and have a little chat with Saunders. Then we'll come back to the hotel. I want to check footage not only of the hotel but the parking lots."

"Leave it to Saunders to make us put in a long night. That man is not cooperative."

"It's people like him that make me question staying a U.S. Marshal." Colton increased their pace toward the parking lot where the rest of the team was waiting with Saunders.

"But if we can take down a child-smuggling ring these long nights will be worth it."

As they left the building, Colton dropped his arm from her waist. Lisette surveyed the lot where the team had parked their various cars around the one Janice and Neil had brought Saunders in. Over half the cars were gone. Couples walked toward their vehicles. She searched among the crowd for any sign of the woman Saunders had danced with, the waiter who had bumped into him or the clown. No sign of any of them.

The velvet coat that matched the costume she wore wasn't warm enough. A cold wind blew from the north and burrowed deep into her bones. There was a chance for snow. But she didn't think that was the reason for the chill. Something went wrong tonight, and she didn't know the full scope of it. She hated loose ends. That was one of the reasons she'd become an FBI agent in the first place.

At the cabin Colton parked behind the car Neil had driven to the masquerade ball and watched as the marshals escorted Saunders inside. Before talking with the man, Colton needed to compose himself and not let Saunders rile him. That wasn't always easy. The guy had a talent for getting under a person's skin.

Lord, give me the patience to deal with this man. I know I don't always have it, but I'm being played. I just know it. What do I do?

"Are you okay?" Lisette asked, her husky voice penetrating the anger beginning to build toward Saunders. He angled his head toward her. The soft light from her open car door revealed worry lines knitting her forehead.

His anger dissipated. "I was just thinking about our witness. It'll be nice when we don't have to deal with him anymore."

"So Saunders isn't going to be your new best friend?"

"Not even if I was desperate."

Lisette laughed. "I'm with you on that one."

The light musical sound caused his stiff muscles to relax. His hands slipped from the steering wheel he'd been gripping like a vise. "Let's get this interview over with. We still have a lot to do tonight."

After placing a call to the team in the cabin, Colton climbed from his car. A light snow began to fall. He felt ridiculous dressed as Romeo. The wind sliced through him. With the tights, he might as well be in shorts. Good thing he'd thought to bring a change of clothes. He grabbed his duffel from the backseat and hurried toward the cabin.

At the door Lisette peered at his bag. "An extra set of clothes?"

Nodding, he knocked on the door. "You look great in your gown. My costume stands out like a neon light in the pitch-black of night."

A faint blush stained her cheeks. From the cold? Or his compliment? She made a point of playing down her beauty. Was she uncomfortable with it? Why?

Those questions fled Colton's mind when he stepped into the toasty warm cabin and faced Saunders. Frowning. Did the man have another expression?

Their witness paced in front of the gas fireplace. "My one night of freedom—something more interesting than a solitaire game—and the evening was cut short."

"This place beats being in prison," Neil grumbled, then went into the kitchen and plugged in the coffee.

"So you weren't happy with the lights going out?" Colton dropped his duffel bag on the floor and covered the space between him and Saunders.

"Why would I be? I had my arms around a beautiful woman, enjoying her company."

"She wasn't your contact?" Lisette sat on the couch, crossing her legs and lounging back as though she didn't have a care in the world.

But if she was anything like him, Colton imagined she was tied up in knots, trying to figure out what really went down tonight. "If she wasn't, who was?"

"She wasn't. At least, I don't think so. She was the pleasure part of this evening." Saunders plopped into a chair close to the fireplace. "I'm not sure when the message was passed to me. Frankly, I thought it hadn't been until I put my hand in my pocket as I was trying to find my way out of the ballroom in the dark."

"So you have no idea who did? The waiter who bumped into you? The man who fought with you? Little Bo Peep?" Suspicious of anything that came out of Saunders's mouth, Colton took a seat on the couch next to Lisette. The scent of coffee perking saturated the small cabin. He would need a lot to stay up this evening and then drive back to the hotel.

"What part of 'I don't know' do you not understand?" Saunders dug into his front pocket and withdrew a wad of paper. "I was gonna read it when I got to the lobby."

"That's okay. I'll take it." Colton leaned forward with his palm out.

"I can't read it?"

"No need to."

Saunders's eyes narrowed to slits as he dropped the crumpled paper into Colton's hand. "The least you could do is read it out loud. You wouldn't have it if I hadn't come to you with the information."

Neil barked a laugh and spilled the coffee in one of the mugs he was bringing to the trio in front of the hearth. "I think you've got it wrong. Remember when you were captured at the warehouse?" After handing Lisette her drink, he went back to the kitchen to get a rag to wipe up the mess.

With his usual glare, Saunders raised his chin. "Still, I'm the reason you have this lead. Remember that when you're looking down your nose at me."

Colton spread out the note, scooting closer to Lisette for her to read it, too. Ignoring Saunders's disgruntled look, Colton swung his attention to her. "What do you think?" He hoped she'd understand his reference to where the baby exchange would take place.

"Not the best place."

"Where? Since I'm gonna be the person to pick the baby up, I think I should know. Who am I gonna tell?"

Colton shifted his gaze to Saunders. "Who said you would be involved?"

"Well, hello, because they're expecting me. You don't think the powers-that-be haven't given the courier a picture of the person he is to hand the child off to?"

"He does have a point," Lisette said in a strained voice, "although I hate the idea of him holding any child."

"Me? I have nephews, and I'm great with them."

Lisette leaned close to Colton and murmured, "Poor boys."

He got a whiff of a light flowery fragrance that reminded him of a field of wildflowers growing not far from his extended-stay hotel. When he jogged, he could smell their scent as he went by.

"Where do we pick up the baby?" Saunders asked, surging to his feet. "I have a right to know."

"Your rights don't involve this. You'll be informed when you need to know the day of the exchange." Colton rose and met Janice halfway to grab the mug she brought him.

"When?" Saunders said in a demanding voice.

"I'll tell you if you tell me what you did when the lights went out."

"I tried to find you. What else was I gonna do? Escape? You had guys on all the exits. Besides, my best chance is to get a clean start somewhere I can't be found. Otherwise, I'm dead. That's a good motive to make sure this all works."

"You would think." Colton sipped the hot drink.

"What's that supposed to mean?"

"You haven't answered my question. Right before the lights went out, you disappeared."

Saunders's face slowly became red, and he made fists at his sides. "My mama didn't raise no dummy. I didn't disappear. *You* did. I swung the lady around and looked toward where you had been and you were all gone. You haven't been listening to me. I couldn't leave if I wanted to. And I didn't." He began pacing in front of the fireplace, opening and closing his hands. "I'm putting my life on the line to get what you need. I deserve some respect."

Colton let him stew for a long moment. There wasn't any reason not to tell Saunders about what was on the paper other than to see how he reacted. Saunders might slip and give him an idea of what was going on. "The baby comes in the day after tomorrow in the morning. No flight number. Just a time for you to meet the person in the baggage claim area."

"How do I know who it is?"

"He'll—or for that matter she'll—know who you are and approach you with the child and will say, 'Do you know a good hotel nearby?' You'll say, 'Any of them are good.' Before the courier will hand over the baby, he'll ask you what the code sentence is."

"What is it, or are you gonna keep me in the dark about it?"

"'Jackson wishes you a happy birthday.'"

"Who in the world thought up this stuff?"

Colton gritted his teeth. The whine in Saunders's voice screeched against his nerves. "You'll have to take that up with Jackson. After all that, the exchange will take place."

Saunders paused, a scowl making his thick eyebrows scrunch together. "Where?"

Colton shrugged. "We'll have to wait and see." The drill of Lisette's gaze pierced through him.

"If it's gonna work, the courier can't be picked up. Otherwise, Jackson will find out. And it can't look like half the people in the area are cops." Saunders prowled from one end of the living room to the other. "Does it say where I'll take the baby?"

"Nope. I'm assuming the courier will tell you that." Colton took another swallow of his coffee while Janice sat at the computer checking the camera shots.

"Snow is coming down." Janice swiveled around in her chair. "You two should head back into town. If our guest remembers anything else, I'll let you know."

"Not tonight. I'm going to bed." Saunders headed across the room to the hallway. "I've got a headache."

When his bedroom door clicked shut, Lisette rose, the same intense expression on her face. "Does he have to be involved in the exchange? Look what happened tonight. He's up to no good."

"That's clear." Colton finished the last few sips of his drink, then put the mug on the counter in the kitchen. "But what? He's been in our custody from the time he was apprehended at the warehouse."

"Not on lockdown. He did get a call before he told you all he wanted to make a deal. Who did he call?" Janice asked.

"From what the marshals said, his lawyer was in court so he decided not to leave a message. At first, he wanted to talk directly to his lawyer, then when he decided to cooperate with us, he thought it best no one knew where he was, even his lawyer." Lisette twirled strands of her hair around her finger.

Was that another sign she was upset, when she didn't have her glasses to fidget with? "I see you've been reading Saunders's file. We'll talk about it on the way to the hotel." A grin tilted Colton's mouth. "I'd rather these two be snowed in with Saunders than all four of us. I'm afraid it could get ugly if there were five of us in this small cabin."

Laughter burst from Janice. "I see you're not sending Neil and me home."

"We're not going home just yet. We're checking out what happened at the hotel first."

"I still think we got the short end of the straw," Neil grumbled as he followed Lisette and Colton to the door.

"We'll be back tomorrow morning to relieve you unless it's a blizzard. What snow I've seen won't stop me. Remember I grew up in Alaska. I'm used to worse." Colton stepped out into the wind, which whipped against him with small flakes falling fast enough to cover his car.

As they hiked the short distance to the Firebird, Lisette said, "I grew up in New Orleans. Until I moved here, I had no idea how deep snow can get. This winter I'm finally getting used to it. That's one reason I have my SUV. The four-wheel drive is great."

Colton slid behind the steering wheel and started the engine. "I know Saunders isn't to be trusted. We'll put protocol in place to keep him in line at the airport. At least I don't see the lights going out there. Besides, the exchange is in the middle of morning, and the baggage claim area has a lot of windows."

"And doors. We'll need all the help we can get. A child's life is involved. Selling a baby is unthinkable."

Colton pulled out onto the highway, the road slick with the fresh snow. Thoughts of St. Louis flashed into his mind. Something sinister was going on there and it had spread out to infect a lot of places. "From what I've read about you, you've worked on a lot of cases involving children. Why?"

"As a teenager I worked at a day care center. At church every Sunday, I took care of the babies. I loved it."

"Then why did you go into law enforcement? Why not become a teacher or something?"

"Because I wanted to be like my…" Her voice faltered, and she went quiet.

At the turn onto the Interstate 70 ramp, Colton glanced at her. Shadows played across her features, but he didn't need to see her face completely. He could read her expression: closed, distant, her gaze slanting away from him. He'd hit upon a sensitive subject she didn't want to discuss, which only made him more curious. He'd heard rumors about her mother. Something happened with her. She'd been on the fast track to the higher echelon in the Bureau, then she'd resigned and disappeared. He'd never liked the politics of an organization so he had steered clear of any discussion with fellow agents he'd known.

Colton merged with the slow-moving traffic on I-70. "When we get to the hotel, the first thing we should do is look at the surveillance tapes."

"And see what their security says about the lights going out."

"Right. I'll take the tapes. You check with security."

Silence fell between them, and Colton decided not to break it. They were temporary partners. Soon this would be over. He'd go for interviews in Dallas and L.A. for positions that were opening up at those offices, and she'd go her own way. They'd probably never work together again, and that was just fine with him. There was something about Lisette that intrigued him, and he didn't want to pursue the attraction.

As Lisette followed hotel security down to the basement below the ballroom to check on the fuse box, she replayed the conversation in Colton's car on the trip from the cabin. She'd almost blurted out why she'd become an FBI agent: her mother. That would have led to a discussion she didn't care to have.

Lisette hadn't talked to her in years. When she'd tried to reach out to her after her mother had been asked to resign, she hadn't wanted to see her or talk to Lisette at first. She'd believed her mom innocent until they had finally discussed what happened to her mother. When Lisette walked away from their last meeting six years ago, she'd felt her mother had done something wrong. Lisette's anger grew as she'd received the cold shoulder within the Bureau and been given the worst assignments. It was clear people thought Lisette was guilty by association. She should forgive her mom. Their relationship had always been rocky because she'd never been able to do enough to earn her mother's approval. But these past years her faith had been affected. The Lord wanted her to forgive; she hadn't been able to bring herself to do so.

The security guard stopped at a fuse box. "Someone tampered with this. Must have caused the lights to go out."

"Who has touched this box since you discovered the cause of the blackout in the ballroom?"

"Just myself when I fixed the problem."

"Then I'll need your fingerprints to rule them out." Lisette stepped up to the panel and began dusting for latent prints. "What did you touch?"

The guard pointed to the door on the box and the fuses involved with the lighting of the ballroom. "That's all."

As she pulled what prints there were off the panel, she said, "You touched here?"

"Yes, ma'am."

Lisette finished her task, but it was beginning to look as though the only set on the fuse box would be the security guard's. If that were the case, that meant it had been wiped clean after the deed had been done. "How accessible do you think this area is for others?"

"It wouldn't be difficult if a person knew what he was looking for and where." The guard retraced his path to the elevator.

"So someone had to have knowledge of the hotel layout?"

"Probably or he would be wandering around. The more he did, the more likely he'd be discovered and questioned. No one was tonight. We do have cameras in various places, but they aren't monitored in real time. So it's possible we missed something."

"We'll need the tapes of this part of the basement for this evening." Lisette exited the elevator on the floor where the hotel security office was located.

As she walked down the corridor toward the room at the end, her high heels clicked against the wood tiled floor. She glanced at her watch. It was after two in the morning. She didn't think she'd be able to sleep much tonight. Images of the masquerade ball kept parading across her mind. Five minutes unaccounted for. What mischief had Saunders been up to? Did he really think they would believe he had been searching for her and Colton?

The guard opened the door to the office and waited for Lisette to enter first. Colton and another man were viewing footage of the main lobby earlier in the evening. "I'll need access to this one, too."

"Also any of the basement area around the fuse box," Lisette said as she took a chair next to Colton.

He looked at her. "Did you find anything interesting?"

"I think the fuse box was wiped clean except for his prints. I only found ones where he touched." She indicated the guard who had accompanied her. "But I will run all the ones I took."

Colton shifted to the security guy next to him. "Please pull that footage up. Start with half an hour before the lights went out."

After a couple of minutes, the corridor leading to the fuse box flashed up on the computer screen. The hotel employee fast-forwarded until a man appeared getting off the elevator. He stopped it to run in real time.

"Do either of you know this person?" Colton asked.

Lisette moved behind him to get a better view while the guard by the door came to her side. The man striding down the hallway, dressed in black slacks, white dress shirt and maroon tie, knew where he was going. No hesitation. No searching a corridor that ran into the one he was taking. He kept his head bent down, away from the camera, as if aware he was being watched. At the box, he opened the panel with a handkerchief and used it to pull the necessary fuses, then he swiped down the area, pivoted and hurried back the way he came. But instead of using the elevator, he took the stairs.

"Are there cameras in the stairwell?" Colton asked, excitement lacing his voice.

"Yes." The security guy next to him brought up the footage of the stairwell and, using different shots, followed the saboteur up to the first floor where he entered a room nearby, then left a moment later with a coat on. As he left the hotel, his face still hidden from view, Lisette bent forward. "Stop. I see something that might help us ID the man." She tapped the monitor. "Zoom in on the front of his jacket. There's something on it."

A clear image of a moose appeared on the screen. "A logo? The writing under the moose is not clear—it's too small from this camera's angle." Colton looked at both men. "Have you seen this before?"

"Actually, I did earlier this evening when everyone was arriving for the masquerade ball," the guard next to Lisette said.

She shifted toward him. "Do you remember seeing this man's face?"

FIVE

Colton rose, facing the hotel security officer whose name, Allen Prince, was plainly displayed on the gold nameplate on his dark navy blue coat. "Anything at all you can remember would be a big help in finding this drug dealer we're looking for." He'd used the explanation to the hotel security staff that he was a U.S. Marshal, heading a team looking for an escaped drug dealer who was supposed to be at the ball.

Prince twisted his mouth. He squinted as though trying to remember. "I saw him when he was getting out of a car. I was off to the side watching the people in costumes arriving for the ball. A limousine service dropped him off."

"Do you remember which company?" Colton glanced back at the computer monitor in the office and could see fuzzy lettering underneath the moose. The distance from the camera and the angle of the shot didn't make the photo clear.

"Sinclair Limousine. Their cars are all white. I might be able to work with a sketch artist. If I saw the guy again, I think I would recognize him."

"But you haven't seen him before today? You don't think he's an employee?"

"He might be. I only work the night shift. I'm not familiar with all the staff who work days."

Colton removed a card. "If you think of anything at all, I want you to call me. I need your address and phone number. I'll send a sketch artist over to your place tomorrow. Once we have a picture of him, we need to circulate it among your employees. This might be our first break."

Prince moved to the desk, jotted his information down on a piece of paper, then handed it to Colton. "I hope you catch the drug dealer."

"So do I," Colton replied, catching Lisette's attention. "It's late. We'll be reviewing the footage from this evening in detail tomorrow, especially with regards to the man in question. Maybe we'll find him in another clip with his face revealed. Thank you two for your cooperation."

"We've never helped in capturing an escaped criminal," the other security employee said.

Colton nodded at the two, then made his way with Lisette toward the door. Out in the hallway away from the office, he released a long breath. "Thankfully they accepted our reason for being here tonight without risking exposing what was really going on with Saunders."

"I've found a lot of security people want to help an ongoing investigation. The info Allen Prince gave us might be just what we need to discover what really went down tonight since Saunders won't be forthcoming."

"We could threaten him with revoking his deal with the government."

"I'm not sure he's smart enough to know what's best for him."

Colton halted at the end of the corridor. "Until today, I would have said the same thing. I think there's more going on in that head of his than he wants us to know."

Her full lips thinned out. "Then that's even more of a reason not to let him be a part of the exchange."

He shook his head, wishing he could prevent that. "Whoever is the courier is expecting him."

"Yes, it's interesting how clear that has been made to us."

He couldn't seem to take his eyes off her mouth, tinted red to match the costume she wore. Tonight she'd worn makeup that emphasized her beautiful features. Usually she played them down. What had caused her to do that? He'd dated women who were gorgeous and had no problem highlighting their assets. Some had even used their beauty to get what they wanted. Lisette was the opposite, and that piqued his curiosity.

At her car, she turned toward him. "What's the plan for tomorrow? We have a lot to work out before the exchange the following day."

"I'll pull in another marshal to guard Saunders with Quinn. Probably Brad. They'll relieve Janice and Neil. We'll meet at the U.S. Marshals' office by eight and make our way through the hours of hotel footage. I only viewed a little of it tonight. We'll specifically be looking for the clown, Little Bo Peep, the waiter who bumped into Saunders on the dance floor and the guy who turned the lights off. Then we'll go out to the airport and case it out. I like to have a plan and then several backup ones."

"I agree. It wouldn't hurt to have someone monitoring the surveillance cameras at the airport when the exchange goes down. I can call an agent at the FBI to help with that."

"Fine. This is going to require a lot of coordination. The airport is crowded, especially at that time of day. This is skiing season, and the snow in the mountains has been good this year."

"If all goes well, this will be over in a few days. That is, if Saunders comes through."

The soft glow of the lights in the parking lot played across her face, drawing his attention to those full lips, sparkling green eyes slanting slightly up, the arch to her eyebrows, her pert nose, the few freckles covered by her makeup. He liked those freckles. In fact, he found he liked both Lisettes—the glamorous one and the professional one.

"I hate to think we're depending on Saunders, but that's often what the U.S. Marshals Service depends on. Criminals like Saunders."

Her chest rose and fell with a deep sigh. "I know. The FBI deals with their share of criminals leading them to other bigger ones."

"Does it ever get to you?" Colton asked as they stood in the middle of the parking lot, a few flakes still falling, the silence from the recent snow making it seem like no one else was around even though a hotel full of hundreds of people was yards away.

"Yes, especially when dealing with a case involving a child."

"Then why do you ask for those cases?"

"Because someone has to and I vowed long ago to protect the children."

"Why?"

Shivering, she hugged her arms against her. "Why not?"

"This isn't the time to talk about it. I need to let you go. Eight o'clock will be here in five hours." But he made a note to ask her again. Each time he saw her defenses go up, his curiosity concerning her deepened. It must be the detective in him. He couldn't afford for it to be anything else. "Good night." He reached around her, brushing his arm against her, and opened her door. "See you in a few hours."

She hesitated. "Does it ever get to *you?*"

"All the time. That's why I turned to the Lord, or I couldn't do this job."

She tilted her head to the right, one corner of her mouth lifting, her eyes softening. "See you at eight."

When she slipped inside, he shut the door and stepped away. He waited until she'd driven away before heading to his car a few rows away. What did that last look mean?

The next evening the lights of the Denver airport faded from view out the side mirror in Colton's Firebird. Lisette relaxed back in her seat, closing her eyes for a moment. She worked hard to gather her thoughts after a long, tiring day watching hours of footage of the hotel from the night before, then coming to the airport to coordinate the security for tomorrow's exchange.

No matter how thoroughly they planned today, Lisette couldn't shake the feeling something bad would happen tomorrow. Chills goose bumped her from head to toe. She rubbed her hands up and down her arms.

"You want me to turn up the heat?" Colton asked as he slipped into the traffic on I-70.

She slid her eyes open and stared out the windshield, glad there was no snow falling. "It wouldn't help. I was thinking about the exchange. I wish we could meet the courier without Saunders."

"If we could, I'd be the first one on board. We want the baby, and we want the middleman. Saunders is our means to both at this time."

"I know. You're not telling me something I haven't said over and over to myself. But Saunders is such a…" She couldn't find the word to describe the creepy, slimy way she felt when around him.

"*User. Predator.* Those are kind words to describe him. In the end he'll get his just rewards."

"But he'll go into WitSec and live a life somewhere safe."

"What I meant is he'll have to answer to the Lord in the end for his sins. That thought is what keeps me going some days when I see people get away with crime. They aren't really. It'll catch up with them."

"Is that what you meant by your faith helping you to do your job?"

Colton glanced toward her. "Yes."

In the dim light of the car, their gazes connected for a second before he looked away, but in that instant she realized she liked him. There was a depth to him that surprised her. He'd seen some evil things in his line of work, and yet he still believed in God. In fact, his job had strengthened his faith whereas she had begun to pull back from hers.

"You've given me something to think about. I'd started to believe the Lord didn't care about the evil that occurred all the time."

"Evil is in our world. It's how we deal with it that's important. Do we let it overtake our lives or do we do our small part to stop it? We all have choices."

Lisette angled toward Colton, the passion in his words washing over her. Free will. She'd forgotten the Lord had given them that.

"I thought we could grab something to eat before I take you back to your car at the office. There's a small café not too far from there that has great food. I'd like to go over what we've discovered today. It helps me to talk it over."

"I often end up talking to myself about the suspects and

leads. It would be nice to talk to someone who will answer me back, and I love finding good restaurants."

Colton took the off ramp. "Good, because I'm starved."

"That's because all we had for lunch was coffee."

"I like coffee. Okay, I love it, but it's better with food or so my stomach tells me."

Five minutes later, he pulled into a parking space next to a redbrick building. As they rounded its side, snow began to fall.

Stepping under the green awning in front, Lisette shook the flakes off her overcoat. "I'm hoping this will stop soon. We don't need to deal with bad weather on top of everything else."

"Bad weather seems to go with Saunders, starting with my trip to the airport in St. Louis. But he didn't seem to appreciate the way I handled the car in that snow."

"He complains about everything. There's not enough mustard on his sandwich. The coffee is too strong. The next day too weak. The list goes on and on."

"Right now a sandwich could be drenched in mustard and the coffee could grow hair. I wouldn't mind." Colton opened the door to Maxie's Café and waved to an older woman across the room. "That's Maxie. She's a jewel."

Maxie approached them as Colton held the chair out for Lisette, then took his seat. "It's good to see you, Colton. You haven't been around for a while. I know it isn't the weather that keeps you away."

"What can I say? Work."

"I'm always reassured that you are hard at work. That means the bad guys are being taken care of." Maxie smiled at Lisette while handing out the menus. "I'm Maxie. Are you a marshal, too?"

"No. FBI. I'm Lisette."

"Is this a date or a big case?" the older woman said with a twinkle in her blue eyes.

"A case. You know me and work." Colton handed her the menu. "I want my usual. You make the best hamburger in Denver. No. The whole state, and I've been thinking about one for the past couple of hours."

"How about you?" Maxie turned her attention to Lisette.

"I love a good hamburger so I'll have what he's having."

"Just so you know, I use buffalo meat for my hamburgers. Okay?"

"I'm game, and I'd like a seltzer to go with it."

Colton waited until Maxie left before pulling out his pad he used to write down information about a case. "Let's see. We identified the type of car the clown left the hotel in. A silver Lexus no more than two years old with a partial plate number 891."

"I'm having an FBI agent run a list of silver Lexus cars with that number on their license plates. That could give us a lead."

"We have a general description of the man—a long hooked nose, brown eyes, about six-foot-three and weighing two hundred give or take ten pounds. I'd like you to work with the sketch artist on the shape of his head, the width of his eyes, high cheekbones. We may need it."

"I can do that tomorrow morning before we head to the cabin to pick up Saunders."

Colton spied Maxie returning with their drinks—a hot steaming coffee for him and the soda for Lisette. "How can you drink something cold with the freezing weather outside?"

"I guess I could ask for hot seltzer, but I doubt it would be as good as a cold one. If I don't switch to something without caffeine, I'll be up all night. I need a good night's

sleep. Tomorrow is going to be long and, I imagine, trying."

"Yeah, even if everything goes smoothly, we'll still
need to deal with an unknown baby and finding the middleman." His gaze snared hers.

For a long moment she didn't want to look away or talk
business. The other customers faded from her consciousness, and it was only Colton and her sharing a dinner. No
case. Just two single people. Suddenly she pulled up short
and tore her look away.

Colton cleared his throat. "The waiter who bumped into
Saunders is the most promising. Neither one of us could
identify him from photos in the employment records of
the waitstaff last night. So who is he?"

"He could still be the last-minute replacement for that
one waiter who called in sick. We should get confirmation
tomorrow of who took the man's place."

Colton took a sip of his coffee, keeping his attention on
the paper in front of him. "Then there is Little Bo Peep.
We've got a good picture of her without her mask in the
lobby. I've got a marshal checking with some people who
attended to see if anyone knows her."

What in the world happened a moment ago? Lisette
wondered. She didn't like losing her focus in the middle
of a case. That could lead to a slipup. She had to do everything perfectly and by the book if she was going to prove
herself. Her career couldn't take anything going wrong.
And Colton had a way of making her attention stray.

"Lisette?"

She blinked and forced her mind back to the task at
hand. "The one we need to find for sure is the man who
turned off the lights. He has to be involved in this some-

how. Was that supposed to be a diversion to allow Saunders to escape? Or someone else?"

"Sinclair Limousine didn't tell us much. They picked him up, then dropped him off at the same downtown corner. No telling where he went after that."

"We got a confirmation from the limo driver on the security guard's take on what the man looked like at least."

"Also we're working on the logo. Big Creek Lodge. There are several in the vicinity. We'll start with them and move outward."

"When I think of moose, I think of Alaska, although I know they're in the lower states, too." She saw Maxie heading to their table with a tray of food. "We may be wasting our time. Everything will go all right tomorrow, and we'll catch the middleman."

"But we want to catch everyone involved in this ring in Denver." Colton sent Maxie a huge smile. "It smells wonderful. If I could afford a cook, I'd steal yours."

Maxie set the plates down in front of them. "If you know what's good for you, you'll back off my cook or I can't be responsible for what the other customers might do."

"You don't have to worry. My pay scale doesn't allow me that luxury. I have to be satisfied coming here." He winked at Maxie, who laughed as she left them alone.

Lisette watched her greet two customers by name.

Colton tossed a look at Lisette. "If you come into this restaurant, Maxie will remember your name and greet you like she's been waiting all day for your appearance. That's part of the charm of this place."

Lisette took her first bite, savoring the smoky flavor of the buffalo burger. "I'd come back just for this. This is delicious."

"I'm glad you like it. We'll have to come back when we finish with this case and send Saunders on his merry way."

"Now that's something to celebrate." She raised her glass and clinked it against his mug.

Fifteen minutes later Lisette sat back, stuffed with an extra-large burger and fried onion rings. "Great ending to a long day."

Colton signaled Maxie for the check. He pulled out his wallet to pay for both meals.

"How much is mine?" Lisette opened her purse.

"This is my treat. You can pay when we come back to celebrate saying goodbye to Saunders."

She thought about protesting. She didn't want anyone to think it was anything but work, but Colton didn't give her a chance. He hurriedly laid the dollar bills down on the checkered tablecloth and stood as though he knew what she was going to do.

"Let's go." He turned away to say good-night to Maxie.

Lisette rose, and Colton started for the door. She paused for a moment to tell Maxie, "Your café is wonderful. I'm glad Colton brought me here."

"Then I hope to see you again. I was kinda surprised to see him with you. He never brings anyone in here when he comes to eat."

She was the first?

Colton waited at the door for her before opening it and letting her leave first. "What did Maxie say to you? You got a funny look on your face."

"She told me you always eat here alone."

"I don't like my dinner being ruined with unnecessary talk. I usually gobble down food except when I come here. I found this café my first month in Denver and probably come at least once a week to eat. It's not far from my place or work."

"It's not that far from my apartment, either. I'm honored you shared it with me." The wind sliced through her heavy coat. Ice pelts stung her face. "This weather doesn't bode well for us."

"This can be normal for February. I'm praying for a beautiful, clear day tomorrow. If not, we'll handle it." He opened the passenger door for Lisette, then rounded the front of his car.

As he did, Lisette thought about this evening. From all she'd learned concerning Colton Phillips, he was a loner. Maxie's statement about Lisette being the first person he'd brought to the café only supported that impression. She knew the other marshals he worked with respected Colton, so why was he a loner? Now that she'd been around him, she realized he was easy to talk to and was a good team leader.

Earlier she'd come close to saying something about her mother. The fact that she'd even wanted to talk about her to Colton alarmed her. She never talked about her mother to anyone. To this day she couldn't understand why her mom had done what she did. When her mother had been blamed for some money missing from a crime scene and then later hadn't backed up her partner, John, who ended up getting killed, she couldn't prove her innocence and ended up resigning from the FBI. No charges were brought against her mom because the money had disappeared. Since she'd been the poster woman for the FBI, illustrating how far and high a female could go in the Bureau, the FBI didn't pursue the investigation. When she'd point-blank asked her mother about the accusations, she told Lisette she'd never taken any illegal money, but when Lisette wanted to know about her partner's death, her mom refused to say anything. How could her mother *not* back up her partner? When Colton climbed into his Firebird, he looked at Lisette as he shut the door. "Are you all right?"

She couldn't answer him honestly without mentioning her mother. She wouldn't do that and dig up all the angst she'd gone through because of her.

"If you're worried about tomorrow, we've done all we can. Think of it as the first step in no longer having to deal with Saunders."

"Thanks for the tip," Lisette finally said, then slammed the lid on her past before it affected her ability to do her job.

I can't keep doing that. I need to somehow forgive my mother, so I can move on and do my job. But how, Lord?

SIX

Colton waited with Lisette in the airport's main terminal for the marshals and local police who were assisting them. Their associates were following passengers with babies from the flights feeding into the west side of baggage claim and the center carousels. The flight with the courier with the baby was arriving at ten o'clock in the morning, but there had been no information on where they might be coming from. Colton and his team had narrowed down the number of incoming flights at that hour to three, with a total of seven passengers traveling with children under the age of two years. One jet had been delayed and would land in half an hour. That gave them some time to see if the courier was on the second plane. They had vetted the first flight, which had arrived ten minutes early. The three passengers with babies didn't approach Saunders and had already left the baggage claim area.

"We're about to leave the secured area of the airport. I'm tracking a man with a baby. Janice is following a woman carrying a child in a car seat. She stopped to go to the restroom." Neil's voice came through clearly into Colton's earpiece.

"Good. We'll follow behind you." Colton looked at Lisette as she listened to the same message he was hearing. "I have Quinn and Brad in place as a skycap as well as Mark, dressed as a custodian. We have to play this as if someone is watching the exchange." He was using two other U.S. Marshals, Brad Worth and Mark Kirkland, besides his team and some local police to cover the exchange.

"I see you. Here we go." Neil emerged from the secured part of the airport, not far behind a man with a baby in a stroller.

Colton drew in a fortifying breath, picked up his carry-on and fell into step next to Lisette. "This should be over soon."

Posing as his traveling companion, Lisette also carried a small bag. When they entered the west side of the baggage claim area, she said, "I hope this is the one, and we don't have to wait for the delayed flight."

"Me, too."

"I hate the idea that Saunders is by himself, not even handcuffed."

Colton spied Saunders, alone, standing between carousel fifteen and the doors that led to the outside. "We have local police outside if he decides to make a run for it. We have to give him a certain amount of freedom, which doesn't set well with me, either."

"I keep having to remind myself where's he going to go. We've got this place locked down. You made that clear to him earlier. I just hope he listened."

"I know. But in spite of all our work to make plans to cover anything that could go wrong, I'm starting to doubt we thought of everything."

Lisette frowned. "We've done what we can. It's out of our control now."

"And in Saunders's and the courier's hands."

"Now I'm beginning to panic, too."

Colton positioned himself several yards to the left of the man with the baby, putting his carry-on on the floor next to him. The conveyor belt began moving. His body tensed when the passenger looked around the baggage claim area. His gaze landed on Saunders for a few seconds but moved on. The man wheeled the stroller closer to the carousel and lifted a piece of luggage off.

When the man with the stroller started for the exit not far from Saunders, Colton picked up his carry-on, facing Lisette while he issued an order to the team. "The first target on flight 453 is on the move. Wearing blue jeans and a heavy tan sweater, he's pushing a stroller and dragging a rolling bag. He's looking at Saunders again. Moving toward him. Keep your distance until the trade takes place. If it does, then, Mark and Brad, you two follow him. We won't apprehend yet. Repeat. Do not approach. We'll put him under surveillance."

The man approached Saunders. "Do you know where the taxi stand is?" came through the mike Saunders wore.

"It should be right outside the door." Saunders pointed in the direction indicated. "If not, I'm sure there's someone who can tell you out there."

"Thanks. This is my first time here and traveling with my child. It isn't as easy as I thought it would be." The father headed for the nearest door.

Colton scanned baggage claim. "The trade didn't take place, but, Officer Middleton, the man with the stroller is coming your way. Note which taxi he gets into."

"You think that guy is the courier?" Lisette asked as they took up their place for the next passenger a carousel down from where Saunders stood.

"Probably not, but he did talk to Saunders."

"He didn't use the correct catchphrases."

"True, but it doesn't hurt to know where he goes. We don't have enough man power to track every person with a child, and it really isn't necessary. I'm only interested in the courier."

"Colton, my woman left the restroom without the car seat and is carrying her baby now. We're almost to the baggage claim," Janice said over the comlink.

"What took her so long? Where's the car seat?"

"She changed a diaper and then stopped at a gate not being used and fed her baby. The car seat is still there."

"Strange. Why leave the car seat?"

"The child was screaming and has been ever since coming off the plane. She appears to be flustered, but it still is odd she left it. I think she's the courier."

"I agree, Janice. Stay as close as you can without being suspicious. Lisette and I are at the carousel next to where the woman will pick up her luggage." Colton peered outside. "Officer Middleton, notify security to pick up the car seat. We don't want anything left unattended."

Lisette turned her back to the incoming crowd of passengers to allow Colton to stare in that direction while carrying on a conversation. She slanted a look toward Saunders. "I sat behind a mom with a baby on my flight back to Denver a couple of months ago. I felt sorry for her."

"The baby or the mother?"

"Actually both. She was trying to keep the baby quiet and got upset when she couldn't. Of course, the situation was made worse with some of the comments by the people sitting around her. Is she here yet?"

"Just came into baggage claim, holding a baby while carrying a diaper bag over her shoulder. She appears harried, as Janice said."

"Believe me, you would be, too, if you'd been dealing

with a child crying on a plane. I don't hear any crying so feeding the baby must have worked."

"She's coming this way. She's searching the crowd waiting for the passengers. She sees Saunders and is hurrying her pace." Suddenly Colton wrapped his arms around Lisette and pulled her against him. "She glanced this way," he whispered into Lisette's ear, the aroma of apples swirling around him as he breathed in the scent of her hair.

"I see her. Her attention is on Saunders."

Colton parted, moving around to watch the exchange. The young woman smiled at Saunders.

"Do you know a good hotel nearby?" The woman asked the question the note indicated the courier would say.

"Any of them are good." Saunders perked up.

She sighed, her shoulders sagging. "Mr. Saunders, you look just like the photo I was given. I wasn't sure it would be that easy." The dark-haired woman's low voice with a slight quaver sounded in Colton's earpiece.

Since not all people involved in the stakeout had direct access to what was transpiring between Saunders and the courier—only his team—Colton said over his comlink, "The exchange is going down." While Lisette kept an eye on the meeting, he turned his back on the pair to give more information. "She is five feet four or five inches, with dark brown hair in a ponytail. She's wearing jeans, a black sweatshirt and tennis shoes. Looks to be between twenty and twenty-five."

Colton moved with Lisette toward the carousel as the last of the baggage came by. In this new position he was behind the lady.

She brought the baby, wrapped in a pink blanket, around for Saunders to get a view of the child. "I was told to ask you for the code sentence before handing over the package."

"Package," Lisette muttered. "She has to know what she's doing. No chance she was duped."

"Jackson wishes you a happy birthday," Saunders said, amusement in his voice.

"Oh, good." The young woman thrust the child into Saunders's arms. "She's been crying a lot."

"What's her name?" Saunders asked.

The woman shrugged. "No one told me. This is her diaper bag with what you need. The phone is inside, and you'll be contacted about where to take her." She looped it over his shoulder, then hurried out the door closest to her.

"Courier is coming out," Colton said into his comlink, then described the lady again. "Brad and Mark, I want you two to follow her. See where she goes. Stay with her and report in. For the time being she will be under surveillance until we make contact with the middleman."

Saunders stared down at the girl in his arms with a silly grin on his face. "I'm heading for the car. I think everything is okay. I haven't seen anyone but you hanging around." He cooed to the baby as he walked outside.

"Heads up. Saunders is going to the car. Don't lose him." Colton scanned the baggage claim area one more time, then followed a few yards behind Saunders.

A black SUV pulled up to the curb with Neil driving. Saunders climbed into the rear seat of the vehicle with Lisette slipping into the car on the other side. She took the child and put her into the car seat facing the back cushion.

Colton passed a set of handcuffs to Saunders. "Put them on. Lisette, check to make sure they are secured."

As she tested the handcuffs, Lisette nodded. "They're fastened."

Colton leaned into the SUV to look at the baby—sleeping with a peaceful expression on her face. She appeared no more than three or four months old with a patch of dark hair and long eyelashes that brushed the tops of her rosy cheeks. "I'll follow you to the safe house. Let me know if he receives a call about where to take the baby."

"Will do." After Colton shut the door, Lisette signaled to Neil to leave.

Colton started for his Firebird parked nearby and slid behind the wheel. Going as fast as he could in the traffic leaving the airport, he kept an eye on the black SUV three cars ahead of him as well as the vehicles surrounding him. He didn't want everything to go all right at the airport only to fall apart en route to the cabin. When he took his left hand off the steering wheel, he flexed it to ease his tense muscles, then he repeated the same thing with the right one. But nothing he did loosened the taut grip tension had on him.

Lisette sat next to the car seat in the back of the SUV, keeping her hand on the baby as though that would protect the child from the man on the other side of the little girl. Visions of her younger sister when she was this age taunted Lisette, threatening her concentration. The little girl scrunched up and wiggled closer to Lisette's hand, still asleep. Just like Lydia used to do when she was trying to get her to sleep—before she died from SIDS and her family fell apart. Everything changed after that. She never saw much of her mother. She worked all the time. The same with her dad until he left them. But for the short time she'd had Lydia as a baby sister, she'd protected her the best she could for a six-year-old.

"She's a cute one." Saunders usual whiny voice morphed into a normal-sounding one. "Can I hold her?"

"No. She stays in her car seat," came out of Lisette's mouth so fast it surprised even her. "She's asleep, and we want her to stay that way unless you want her to cry. Didn't you hear the woman say she's been crying a lot?"

"I'm good with children."

Chills shivered up her arms and flashed through her whole body. The very idea he dealt with any baby made her skin crawl. "Then why are you involved in a child-smuggling ring?"

"To make money. I have nothing against kids, and the ones we sell go to parents who really want them. They pay a lot to have them."

"Everyone? You know for sure?" Sarcasm dripped off each question.

He glared at her. "When you haven't done anything wrong, then you can say something. I supply a service to couples who can't have children."

Her stomach roiled, bitter acid swelling into her throat. She swallowed hard and studied the passing scenery. This assignment with Saunders should be over soon—at least the part where she had to deal with the lowlife. She would take great pleasure in catching Jackson and helping to bring this child-smuggling ring down.

When Neil exited the interstate, she watched the traffic behind them to make sure Colton was still there and no one else was following them. With her muscles aching from holding herself stiff for so long, she forced herself to relax back against the cushion, thinking about the day they'd bring the ring to justice. She'd been wound so tightly the whole morning, waiting for something to go wrong at the airport. She spied Colton taking the same off ramp, not far behind them.

The little girl stirred beneath her hand, her eyes opening. The child stared at Lisette, who leaned over the car seat. Her tiny features screwed up as though she were going to start crying.

"Hi, sweetie. You're safe now. I'm not going to let anyone hurt you." The soft, calm tone of her voice seemed to soothe the baby.

The child locked her attention on a necklace around Lisette's neck and reached up with her fat fingers to touch it. The sunlight streamed through the window and gleamed off the gold heart.

But when the child pulled on the chain, Lisette smiled. "I can't let you have this. I'll find something more appropriate for you to play with when we get to the cabin." She raised her head when Neil made a turn onto the gravel road that led to the safe house. "We're almost there."

"You got a kid or something?" Saunders cut into her conversation with the little girl.

"Or something."

"What's that supposed to mean?"

"It's none of your business."

"Well, la-di-da." His mouth settled into his usual frown. "Who do you think you are?"

"I'm Special Agent Sutton, serving on your security detail. Remember that when your previous employer comes after you." The words tumbled from her mouth before she could censor herself.

Up ahead half a mile, the black SUV Neil drove took the road to the cabin. As Colton neared the turnoff for the safe house, a red Ram truck sped up behind him and passed him. At the same time a dark gray Suburban came toward him in the opposite lane. The driver of the Suburban slammed on his brakes to avoid colliding into the truck on his side of the highway. The thin layer of snow caused the car to fishtail, sliding toward Colton. With quick reflexes, he steered his Firebird onto the shoulder of the road while easing up on the gas.

The red truck slowed, as though the driver was making sure no one was hurt, then he drove away, disappearing around a curve a few yards past the gravel drive. The man in the Suburban righted his car, waved at him and continued south on the highway. Colton exhaled a heavy sigh, counting his blessings. A wreck wasn't on his to-do list.

He pressed down on the accelerator, but slowed when he reached the turnoff. Suddenly out of the corner of his eye, the red Ram truck came barreling around the curve straight for him.

Neil pulled up to the cabin. "We're home." He parked the car in front of the cabin. "And it's only noon. I feel like I've been up for twenty-four hours."

"Yeah, you got me up early enough. I'm taking a nap. Wake me if Jackson calls." Saunders reached down on the floor with his cuffed hands, picked up the diaper bag and shoved it toward Lisette's feet.

Neil slid from the SUV first and came to Saunders's door to open it. Lisette scooted out of her side, released the baby from the car seat, then grabbed the bag and slung it over her shoulder. She looked toward the road. Colton should be here any minute. He wasn't far behind them.

The little girl began to squirm, fussing. "I'm going to get her inside and see if she needs her diaper changed." She hurried toward the cabin while Neil escorted Saunders.

Inside, Lisette disarmed the security system, her gaze sweeping the living area and kitchen. Everything was the same as they left it.

When the baby started fussing and wiggling, Lisette headed for the couch. "I need to take care of her."

"I'll check the bathroom and bedroom." Neil led the way down the hall, peering into the small bathroom then moving toward the single bedroom to make sure it was secure. Saunders followed, still handcuffed.

The child's cries increased.

"Sweetie, I'm right here." She laid the child on the couch. "I won't let anything happen to you," she said in a singsong voice.

The sound of Lisette's voice didn't calm her. The baby still wailed, a piercing noise that bounced off the walls of the small cabin. Her face reddened, her tiny hands clenched.

"I'm hurrying." She confirmed the diaper was soaking wet and dug through the bag for another.

Through all of this the child continued to scream. Her sister used to do the same thing. Her cries drowned everything else, forcing a person to see to her needs before doing anything else. Rushing as fast as she could, she grasped a diaper then searched for the wipes.

A crashing sound came from the bedroom. Lisette jerked up and twisted toward the short corridor that led in that direction. She snatched up the bawling baby and placed her on the floor where she wouldn't roll off. Straightening, Lisette clasped the handle of her gun and swiveled toward the hallway.

Just inside the living room, Saunders stood beside a large burly man who had a gun pointed at her.

Sneering, Saunders sauntered farther into the cabin's

living room and glanced at the baby by Lisette's feet. "If you're smart you'll pull your weapon out slow and easy, then place it on the floor and slide it to me, using your foot."

Heart hammering against her rib cage, Lisette did as instructed, not wanting to put the child in any danger. "What you're doing isn't smart. You'll be hunted by the U.S. Marshals Service and your not-so-happy employer. You'll have to look over your shoulder for the rest of your life."

One eyebrow lifted as Saunders plucked the diaper bag off the couch. "I'm flattered you care about my well-being, Lisette, but I have no intentions of living a substandard life working for minimum wage under the government's watchful eye."

"It beats prison or death."

Saunders cackled, a sound that grated down Lisette's spine. "That's what I like about you, your cheerful outlook on life." He waved at the baby. "Pick her up and bring her to me. Remember my friend behind me has his gun pointed at you and has orders to shoot if you cause any problems. Otherwise, I'll leave you like Marshal Simms, tied up but alive. I must say, he might be in a little worse shape."

"What have you done?" She hadn't heard a shot, and there wasn't a silencer on the gun in the bulky guy's hand.

"My friend had to knock him out when he came into the room. His head might be hurting, but that's all."

As slow as she could, she knelt next to the little girl playing with the skirt on the couch; now that her diaper had been changed she seemed happy and content. Lisette picked up the baby and rose, remembering her words to the child only a moment ago about her being safe now. "Are you taking her?"

"Why, of course. She's my ticket out of here."

Lisette held the child close to her chest. "Take me instead of her. I won't cry, demand to be fed and have to have my diapers changed."

"True, but you aren't worth the thousands of dollars I need to escape and disappear. Baby C is."

"You had a good deal. No prison time. A new life." She fought to keep desperation from her voice. Calm logic might work.

"If I did anything wrong, I'd be locked up for the original crime plus any new ones. No way. I don't like restraints on my activities like that. It's like living in a kind of prison. Who knows what things I'd like to do in the future." Saunders stepped in front of her and snatched the baby from her arms. "Besides, I'd be a fool to turn on the people running the child-smuggling ring. Probably dead, too. I'm getting out of here and as far away as I can."

The urge to protest overwhelmed her, but she clamped her lips together. It would do no good. If she kept him talking, Colton might arrive and be able to prevent Saunders from escaping. "So what happened on the way to St. Louis's airport was a planned escape, after all?"

"Yes, but the ice storm hit and messed it up."

"How did your people know where you were?"

"My call before I went into the WitSec Program set everything in motion."

"Your friend there knew about this cabin and its security code from when the lights went out at the masquerade ball?"

"You're one smart lady. It's not hard to see a code when it's punched in, and I read road signs on the way here so the cabin wasn't hard to explain how to get to. I didn't have to say a word at the ball. When the lights went out, I passed my own note to my cohort there with that information. That and it gave my contact at the ball a chance to leave."

"Who was it?" *Where is Colton? Did something happen to him? Or is he outside waiting for them to leave to take them down?*

"You ain't getting that from me." Saunders pulled a small tracking device from his pocket. "I had this on me since the ball, the same type as the one I had in the car to St. Louis airport. I had to leave that one in the car, and this morning I left this tracking device at the cabin so my friends knew exactly where it was."

"Friends?"

"I have another helping me. Do you think I wouldn't take care of Colton, too?"

A hot knot jammed her throat. "What did you do?"

"I caused a delay. Not sure, though, how bad he was hurt. Oh, well." Saunders shrugged. "Sometimes there are casualties." He nodded toward the bulky man behind him.

King Kong came toward her, only pausing long enough to give Saunders his weapon. The gorilla pulled plastic ties out of his coat pocket and gestured for her to turn around. When she did, he yanked her arms behind her and fastened the restraint around her wrists, then he shoved her down on the couch and bound her feet.

Saunders started for the front door with the baby beginning to fuss again. He told her to shut up and that only made it worse.

Lisette bit her lips, worrying about the child with Saunders. Worrying about Neil and how badly hurt he was. Worrying about Colton, who should have arrived by now unless something did happen.

Lord, please protect the baby, Neil and Colton. They're in Your hands. I can't...

"Oh, by the way, I've changed my mind." Saunders turned at the door. "I don't want to leave here and have you immediately get free and call for help." He nodded toward King Kong standing beside Lisette.

Before she could open her mouth to say anything, the butt of the gun came crashing down onto her skull. She slumped to the side, colliding with the softness of the couch cushion.

All Colton saw was red as the truck barreled toward him. He immediately reacted and stomped on the gas, but the driver of the Ram must have anticipated his tactics because a second later the pickup smashed into the side of his Firebird, T-boning it. The crashing sounds of the collision drowned out the rat-a-tat of his heart beating. The exploding air bag followed, its impact forcing him back against his seat with a punch that knocked the breath from him.

The world spun before his eyes. Coughs racked him. He sucked in the fine white powder from the air bag, causing more coughs to rack his body.

Then he felt another jolt as the truck rammed him again, pushing him off the road and into a ditch. Pain streaked up his legs. His car sat at an angle. Through the haze and spinning terrain, he realized he was hanging on the edge of the ditch, teetering. Any movement could send him crashing to the bottom of the six- or seven-foot trench.

Another shove came. His Firebird toppled over into the ditch. A bolt of pain threatened his consciousness. He opened his eyes to find himself hanging upside down with the seat belt the only thing holding him above the water seeping in through a broken window.

He searched his dazed mind for a picture of the gully.

How much water had been in it this morning? Inches or feet? It kept rising toward the top of his head.

He wiggled, trying to find the buckle to undo his seat belt. But before he could, the top of his car slipped down the slope, and icy cold water rushed in from both sides.

SEVEN

Fighting with the seat belt, Colton finally released the latch and plummeted the few inches into the icy water in his car. His left shoulder took most of the impact with the roof of his Firebird. His body ached and cold burrowed deep into his bones, but neither was important at the moment.

The only thing he focused on was getting out of the car and to the cabin. He fumbled for his cell phone, but it wasn't in his pocket. He searched the water and found it submerged. Useless. After trying it in desperation, he tossed it away, pouring all his energy into getting out of the vehicle.

The shattered driver's side window, although scrunched, was his only way out. He kicked out the rest of the glass, then wiggled through the narrow opening, cold water lapping at him. Shivers shuddered down his length. He kept going.

A vision of Lisette flashed into his mind. His heartbeat thumped against his chest.

Lisette needed him. Neil and Saunders. The child.

Halfway out of the car, he paused to listen. No gunshots. That was a good sign, wasn't it? He resumed his struggles, more determined than ever to get to the cabin before someone was hurt. Before they lost Saunders and the baby.

Free, he shoved himself to his feet, using the upside-down car as support. His legs weak, he clutched the bottom of the driver's side door. Light-headedness attacked him, his sense of balance precarious. He took several composing breaths of the frigid air that seemed to freeze his lungs. Wet, cold, with his whole body throbbing as though he'd taken a beating and lost, Colton slogged through the six-inch-deep water with a layer of ice on top to the slope of the trench. Using the root of a tree, he pulled himself up onto the gravel road and surveyed the area.

Where was the red truck?

Gone? Or at the cabin? He rose as quickly as he could. His vision spun before his eyes, and he shut them for a few seconds.

He took a step, then another. Still standing, he deemed that a positive thing and increased his pace. By the time he rounded the bend and saw the cabin, he was jogging, his body protesting the jarring motion.

But he didn't have a choice. No cell phone. No help on the way. He was it. Within yards of the black SUV parked in front of the safe house, the door to the cabin flung open and out dashed Saunders with a pink-blanketed bundle in his arms and an even bigger man behind him.

Immediately the giant spotted him and, lifting his gun, squeezed off a shot before Colton could dive for cover, pulling his own weapon out of the holster. Pain seared through his arm. He scrambled for cover behind a fallen tree and returned fire, making sure he shot to the far right, away from the baby but he hoped close enough to stop Saunders.

Still holding the baby, Saunders ducked behind the car,

opening the driver's door. The other guy shot a few more rounds, then climbed into the back of the SUV.

The huge man rolled down the window and aimed his weapon out of it. More gunshots pierced the air, echoing through the otherwise quiet. The engine started. With Saunders in the front with the baby, Colton couldn't risk returning fire by taking out the driver. He crouched behind the log while bullets pelted the trunk.

Then suddenly it was silent—as if the giant was out of ammunition or reloading.

The sound of the tires crunched on the gravel. Colton popped up to see if he could shoot out the tires before Saunders drove away.

The guy in back was waiting, his gun aiming at Colton as the SUV moved forward.

Gunshots rang out. A bullet whizzed by Colton. Then another. This one hit him, followed by a second one, sending him falling backward onto the ground.

Crack. The sound punctured Lisette's blackness, demanding she do something, but a clanging pounded against her skull. Over and over. Sending pain fingering out to her whole body.

Then through that intense sensation, she realized her cheek lay on something soft and cushiony. She squeezed her eyes as though that action would help her remember what happened. But when she tried, she met with a blank wall.

One eyelid popped opened, then the other. It took a moment to focus. Slowly a massive coffee table with magazines and a deck of cards on it filled her vision. The throbbing in her mind clouded her thoughts. Then she latched on to a mug near the edge of the table. Hers. She'd used it.

When? Where?

All of a sudden her memory flooded back, and she bolted up on the couch. The movement pierced through her brain like a hot poker. She immediately groaned and fell facedown on the cushion. She stayed still for a moment to quiet the elephants tap-dancing in her head, then rolled onto her side, her hands tied behind her back.

Saunders and his cohort were gone with the baby. She had to do something. She struggled to sit up, being careful not to make too many sudden, jerky moves. In a seated position, she shouted several times, "Neil, are you all right?"

Nothing. Concern mushroomed in her. Neil wasn't answering. Colton hadn't arrived. Neither was a good thing. She needed to call for help. Her cell was in her front pants pocket. Leaning forward, she tried to bring her clasped hands around to that side to retrieve it. Five inches separated her fingers and the pocket.

Okay. She'd bring her hands around to the front of her. She fought to get her bottom through the loop her arms formed behind her. They weren't long enough for her to do that. She might as well have hit a ten-foot wall with no way over it.

She lifted her head and searched the living area for something to use to cut the heavy plastic ties. Her gaze fastened onto the landline by the computer. She'd forgotten about that. The hit on the back of her skull must have really done a number on her.

After she scooted to the edge of the cushion, she rocked and pushed herself to her feet. Then she hopped to the table where the phone was. When she managed to knock the receiver onto the tabletop, she turned with her back to it and fumbled to hit the right numbers—9-1-1—while peering behind her.

She bent close to the mouthpiece when the operator came on. After explaining the emergency and the cabin's location, she told the woman she couldn't stay on the line but would leave the receiver off the hook.

She had to see about Neil. Again she yelled out to him, but there wasn't any reply.

Her chest felt tight with each inhalation of air as though a plastic tie was surrounding her torso and Saunders had pulled the restraint taut. Her heartbeat thundered in her head as she bounced her way to the bedroom, praying Neil and Colton were all right. The jarring up and down movement was like a gong being struck over and over inside her skull.

In the hallway, her foot tangled with the other, and she went down, crashing against the wall. Pain swamped her, nearly sending her into the black void hovering in the background. She didn't know if she had it in her to stand. Instead, she belly crawled toward the open door.

Creeping forward, she finally rounded the doorjamb and peered into the bedroom. Only a couple of feet away lay Neil, blood oozing from a head injury. Was he alive?

Through the haze Colton heard a car being gunned and the sound of gravel spewing probably from beneath tires. Lying on the ground, he groaned. His chest hurt. He lifted his head slightly and glanced down his length. Two bullet holes in his coat riveted his attention. Even wearing a bulletproof vest, the punch of the gunshots had bruised his chest.

Saunders, with the baby, was gone.

Escaped.

He labored to his feet, gripping a nearby tree trunk to hold himself upright until he got his bearings. He felt as if he'd been flattened by a Mack truck, then it came back to repeat the action.

Trudging toward the cabin, he needed a phone to get help. He needed to find Lisette and Neil. He refused to think the worst. His steps quickened as his mind cleared, but each rise of his chest when taking a breath flooded his body with pain. He tried inhaling with as little movement of his torso as possible but, with the higher altitude, that caused light-headedness. He endured the pain in order to function.

When he entered the safe house and clutched the door-jamb, he surveyed the living room. Empty. His pulse increased its rate as he charged toward the short hallway and spied the open door.

"Lisette. Neil." He rushed into the room and came to a halt, nearly tripping over Lisette, sprawled on the floor a few feet from Neil. His heart lurched, his gaze frozen on Lisette. What if she were—

Kneeling next to her, he checked her pulse. Beating. Strong. He took out his pocketknife and cut the plastic ties around her hands and ankles, then moved to Neil to see if he was alive.

Lisette moaned behind him. He glanced back at her as he put his fingers on the side of Neil's neck.

"Is he alive?" Lisette shook out her arms, then pushed up.

"Yes. But he has a nasty wound at the back of his head."

"That was Saunders's buddy. He knocked me out with the butt of the gun. That's what happened to Neil probably."

Colton stood. "I need to call for backup and a couple of ambulances."

"I already called for backup. I'm fine. We only need one ambulance…." She paused when her gaze latched on to his left arm. "You've been shot! We need two, then."

"It's a scratch. Hurts and is bleeding but that's all." Okay, his arm and chest burned and throbbed, but he didn't have time to be wounded.

"That's all. Have you looked at your coat sleeve?" Lisette crawled closer to Neil to check on him.

"Do you have your cell phone?"

She slid it out of her front pocket and handed it to him as the sound of sirens filled the air.

That evening Colton entered Lisette's hospital room. "I hear they're keeping you and Neil overnight. Actually, Neil will be here longer."

"Yeah, his knot is bigger than mine." She attempted a smile that faded almost instantly, a dull ache pounding against her skull, the medication the doctor gave her slowly starting to take effect.

"He had me worried at the cabin. He'll be out of commission for a while."

"He'll be okay, won't he?" Lisette shifted on the bed, the movement reminding her why she was in the hospital.

Colton settled into the chair near the bed, scooting it a little closer. He winced.

"How's your arm?"

"It's okay. The bullet grazed my arm. That's all. They cleaned it and bandaged it up. My bruised ribs are entirely another matter, but neither will keep me from finding Saunders and Baby C."

"Baby C?"

"She arrived at Denver Airport at Concourse C. It seemed as good a name as Jane Doe."

"Where did the plane come from?"

"Houston originally with a few stops between there and Denver. How are you doing?"

"I'll be on the job tomorrow as soon as they release me from the hospital. I have a mild concussion, but the pain meds will keep the tapping elephants in my head quiet enough for me to help you find Baby C. And when I get my hands on Saunders, he's going to regret taking her." She remembered the smug look on the man's face and frowned. "He told me she was his ticket out of here. I tried to get him to take me as a hostage, but apparently I might be too much trouble. It's obvious he hasn't been around children, especially babies." Her laugh held little humor. Worry nibbled at her composure. "What if Saunders harms the child?"

"If she's his ticket out of Denver, then he'll make sure she stays alive and in good condition."

Lisette studied Colton's expression. Deep in his blue eyes, she saw the same concern she had. "Yeah, that's what I was thinking." More like praying. "He had been planning this escape from the very beginning. He told me he wasn't a fool to turn in the people running the ring."

"Then he knew who they were?"

"I don't know if he did. I think he knew more than he was saying, though. I feel like we've wasted the past week on the man." Had they wanted this to work so badly that they didn't see what Saunders was really up to?

"I'm not ready to call it a bust. A sheriff deputy found the black SUV a mile from the cabin on a dirt road off the highway and a police officer in Denver located the red truck, abandoned in a warehouse area. It had been stolen from a man who lived outside Boulder. The crime lab is combing through it for any evidence. I'm praying they find something."

"I'll join you on that. We need a break. If he's using Baby C as his ticket out of here, I have a feeling he'll be arranging to sell her to whomever wanted the child in the first place."

One of Colton's eyebrows arched. "Cut Jackson out?"

"What if there wasn't anyone called Jackson and Saunders was the middleman?"

"It's possible. He went to a great deal of trouble to play dumb."

"Which means he has something to hide. I do know the huge man who was waiting in the cabin for us to return was following his orders. Also at the masquerade ball one of the reasons the lights went out was so Saunders could give his contact the directions to the cabin and the security code."

"That's how his cohort found the cabin. Saunders told him. It's hard to keep someone safe when they don't want you to."

Lisette reached toward her plastic cup with water on the end table. "He had no intentions of taking the government's deal."

Colton beat her to it and picked it up, then gave it to her. "I need you at one hundred percent tomorrow. We'll be tracking down which person at the ball was the contact."

The cold water sliding down her throat relieved the dryness in her mouth momentarily. "The clown, the waiter, Little Bo Peep or someone entirely different?"

"I'm hoping it's one of those three. Quinn and Janice will be looking for the man who turned out the lights. We found where his coat came from. A ski lodge not far from Denver. It's a coat their employees wear in winter."

"That might lead us somewhere. I haven't seen the sketch yet. How detailed is the description the security guard and limo driver gave the artist?" She yawned. The doctor had given her something to sleep, and it was affecting her.

"Not bad. Maybe someone will recognize the person at the lodge." Colton rose. "The nurse outside warned me you might not be awake when I came up here. We'll talk tomorrow. I'll be here to pick you up in the morning."

"What about your car?" She hadn't seen it in the ditch because she was in the back of an ambulance, but he had told her it probably was totaled.

"I've rented a Jeep for the time being. When I can, I'll buy a new car. My Firebird is gone, and Saunders will answer for that, too."

"Look out anyone who gets between a man and his car."

"We've known each other a week, and you know me so well. Good night."

When Colton left, Lisette relaxed back and closed her eyes, his last words teasing her. She knew the kind of law enforcement officer he was—thorough, dedicated and protective—but the person beneath that professional facade he presented to the world was a stranger to her. And yet, with what they had gone through together recently, she wanted to know that man. What made him hold himself back from others?

The next day Colton watched Lisette stroll out of a two-story building of stone and glass where her apartment was. Seeing her lifted his spirits after a night tossing and turning, in pain but mostly upset with himself for what went down. He'd gone over and over the scenario, trying to figure out what he could have done differently. Finally at five in the morning, he punched his pillow several times and decided losing any more sleep would only compound his problems. He couldn't change the past. He had to look forward. He would find Baby C. End of story.

The sun shone on the snow-covered ground. The main streets were clear and the secondary roads were passable, especially in the four-wheel drive Colton had rented. This was a good day to start fresh.

When Lisette climbed into his dark green Jeep Grand Cherokee, she smiled. "I appreciate you bringing me by my place to change clothes. You should have come in."

"Another time." He hadn't because it would have made their connection more personal when he saw where she lived—what her possessions were. He learned a lot about a person from seeing their home.

When he had seen her lying on the cabin floor, he didn't like what he'd begun to think. What if something had happened to her? In that moment he realized he cared for her. He needed to shut down those feelings before he began picturing himself staying in Denver to get to know her better.

"Where are we going first?" Lisette's question interrupted his thoughts.

"To pay the clown—aka Harold Freeman—a visit at his job."

"What does he do?"

"He's a plastic surgeon."

"You're kidding!" Lisette's laughter sprinkled the air.

Its sound sent a wave of merriment through him. He'd needed that. "I wonder if he started a fight with Saunders in order to drum up some business. Break his nose. Then fix it."

"Wasn't he the one minus a nose?"

"True," he said with a chuckle, stopping at a red light. "He doesn't work far from you."

"Have you tracked the waiter or woman?"

"We're going by the hotel to talk to the kitchen staff after Dr. Freeman."

"If he wants a second job, I hope he doesn't apply at a circus. Clowns are supposed to entertain, not detain a person."

"I don't think Dr. Freeman is the person we're looking for, but while I'm interviewing him, I want you to have a look around. He works at a high-end medical center where the well-to-do go. Those people can afford to pay a lot of money for a child. If Saunders is looking for money to help him disappear by selling Baby C, then maybe Dr. Freeman could be involved somehow. Time is ticking down."

"I know. I've worked on a number of kidnappings."

"I'm banking on the child being kept alive because of her value to Saunders. I don't want to miss anything like what…" He couldn't bring himself to say it out loud. He should have been able to prevent yesterday. Somehow.

"What happened at the cabin wasn't your fault."

"Then whose fault was it?" He locked gazes with Lisette.

Her mouth firmed. "Saunders's and his cohorts'. I wouldn't put it past Saunders to have written that message from the contact, and there was no one giving him one at the ball—just a tracking device. He had access to paper and pen at the cabin. That's what he used to pass on the security code."

"Either way there was someone at the hotel besides the man who had turned out the lights that helped Saunders. We have to find that person."

He drove into a large parking lot in front of a ten-story building with a sign that read Wellington Medical Center.

Colton walked into the lobby first and went to the information kiosk to find the floor where Dr. Freeman's practice was located. He stepped on the elevator, punching the number four and then turning around. Lisette had waited a moment before she entered the building. As the doors closed, she came into the medical center and strolled to the security guard on duty.

Colton exited on Dr. Freeman's floor, his double doors across from the elevator when Colton got off it. He went into the office and headed to the receptionist desk. He stuck his hand into his pocket for his wallet. "I'm here to talk to Dr. Freeman."

"Do you have an appointment?"

"No, but—"

"I'm sorry. He doesn't have any openings today. In fact, the whole week."

Colton flipped open his wallet, and the young woman's eyes grew round as if he were going to bribe her to see the doctor. He showed her his badge. "I'm here in an official capacity. I need to see him. Now."

The twentysomething lady shot to her feet. "He's with a patient. I'll take you to his office, and he'll be in when he's finished."

Following the receptionist, Colton asked, "How long will that be?"

"I'll let his nurse know you're waiting. I'm sure he'll be in shortly." She opened the door at the end of a long hall.

He stepped inside and inspected the room. He immediately discovered the reason Dr. Freeman went to the masquerade ball dressed as a clown. His office held a collection of Emmett Kelly figurines among the medical books on the shelves behind a massive mahogany desk. Sunshine poured into the place through a bank of windows along the south wall. No pictures of a family anywhere made Colton wonder if the doctor was single. Fifty years old and he currently didn't have a wife?

He wasn't sure why he was curious. It probably had nothing to do with the case, but it still nagged him. Because he was thirty-six and no prospects of getting married in his future? Why was he even thinking that?

He shook the thought of marriage and age out of his mind. But as he prowled the office, another question teased him. Did Lisette date? Had she been married before? Was she involved seriously with someone? In the past he'd never asked a partner that, but the urge to discover the answers to those questions was strong.

What in the world was wrong with him? He paused at the windows overlooking the parking lot, searching for his rental. Anything to take his mind off where his thoughts were going.

What was keeping the doctor?

He glanced at his watch and laughed. Five minutes since he'd come into the room. This was why he avoided getting too close to anyone. That person began to occupy his thoughts more than his job. When getting out of his wrecked Firebird, Lisette was the first one he thought of— not the baby, not the witness he was protecting, not the other marshal. But Lisette. He'd fought to get to the cabin because of her. That realization stunned him.

The door opened, and Dr. Freeman came into his office. "My nurse said you needed to talk to me. Why in the world would the U.S. Marshals Service want to see me?"

Colton shook the image of Lisette from his thoughts and focused on the doctor, who was dressed in black slacks and a white shirt with a charcoal gray tie on, distinguished looking—a far cry from his clown costume. "I'm here following up on an incident that occurred at the masquerade ball a few days ago."

"What incident? Do I know you?"

Colton ignored the second question and answered the first with, "The fight with the pirate."

The doctor eased into his chair behind his desk, leaning back in it. "Why in the world do you care about a disagreement that turned ugly? Frankly, I'm surprised by my behavior. I drank a little too much that evening and took offense at that man's behavior."

"What did he do? I was there, but it was dark so I wasn't aware of anything."

Dr. Freeman cocked his head. "Why is it any business of yours?" The curious tone in his question took the sting out of it.

"I'm looking into anything unusual that happened that night at the ball. I'm on a case involving an escaped drug dealer."

A smile split the doctor's face. "I could see that rat being involved."

"You know the pirate?"

"Well, not really, but he moved in on my date. I couldn't believe my good fortune when Hannah Adams asked me to the masquerade ball. I'd been trying to take her out for the past four months."

"How did he move in on your date?"

"Before going to the party, I took her out to dinner. Since we were dressed in costumes, I had arranged to have a private room at a five-star restaurant set aside for us. I spared no expense."

"Dressed as a clown?"

"That's what she liked about me, or at least that's what she said. I often entertain the children at the hospital. She knew that and asked me to dress as a clown. I was thrilled and did. Anyway, we were late to the ball, which didn't set well with Hannah. The dinner took longer than expected and then we hit some traffic. When we arrived, she danced with me one time, then disappeared. The next time I see her, she's holding on to the pirate, gushing all over him. I lost it."

"Was she dressed as Little Bo Peep?"

"Yes. She looked so cute...." His voice faded as the doctor stared to the side, lost in thought.

Colton cleared his throat.

Dr. Freeman blinked and sat up straight. "Where were we? Oh, yeah. After the lights went out, I totally lost her in the crowd. When I searched for her, I saw that pirate and wanted to know where she was. We had words, and before I knew it, I took a swing at him."

"How do you know Hannah Adams?"

"She works for the fertility clinic in this building. She's a nurse."

"Did you find her? Take her home?"

His eyebrows scrunched together. "No, and she has been avoiding me since then. I don't know what happened."

Colton rose. "I won't keep you. I know you have patients to see. I'd like to ask you to keep my visit confidential. Not to mention it to Hannah Adams or anyone else."

His eyes widened. "Is she involved with the drug dealer?"

"No, but the fewer people who know about our investigation, the better it is. The drug dealer is a very dangerous man."

Dr. Freeman walked with him to the door. "Sure. I understand. Anytime you can put a drug dealer behind bars is a good day. I hope you find him."

"Me, too. Thank you." Colton shook the doctor's hand, then left his office.

As Colton rode the elevator to the first floor, his thoughts spun with myriad questions. His first impulse was to charge over to the fertility clinic and interview Hannah Adams immediately. But in the back of his mind, something nagged at him. If she were the contact, what repercussions would happen if he interviewed her right now? He needed information on her—and the fertility clinic, a perfect place to find prospective parents. He wanted Saunders badly. He was determined to do this right. A baby was at stake.

He found Lisette in the lobby, her eyes sparkling with excitement.

"What did you find out?" he asked, her excitement contagious.

"There's a fertility clinic in this building. It's the whole second floor and I saw a woman get on the elevator not long after you who could have been Little Bo Peep. I know she wore a mask, but the way she walked and something I can't put my finger on made me think it could be her. The elevator she rode stopped on the second floor."

"Let's go. I'll tell you on the way to the hotel about Hannah Adams."

While Colton went to talk with the security staff, Lisette sat in the office of the manager of the kitchen and waitstaff. "I need a list of the waiters on duty a few nights ago at the masquerade ball with a photo ID. We checked once and the photos were of the people who were scheduled to work that night. I need to know if there were any last minute substitutions."

"May I ask why?"

"It's a case I'm working on, and I'm not at liberty to give you any details."

The older man with thinning hair shifted toward his computer and punched in some keys. "There were three who worked the night of the ball who filled in for someone sick that night. Let me see who is here today and who is off."

"We're only interested in the men."

"The three are men." The manager continued to type and brought up a schedule on the screen. "I can pull up each one's photo if you wish, and if the person is here, I can get him."

"Yes, please." Lisette came around to stand behind the man while he went through the pictures of the waiters.

On the last one, Lisette saw the staff member who might have been involved with Saunders. She zeroed in on the man's name. "Is Tom Parks here today?"

"Yes. He's working a luncheon in an hour."

"I'd like to talk to him."

The manager rose. "I'll get him, and you may use my office to talk to him. I have to check on the progress with the luncheon, anyway."

She smiled. "I appreciate your help."

While the man went to bring Tom Parks to the office, Lisette paced, running through the leads and what they had discovered so far. The clown didn't seem to be involved with Saunders, but she'd learned never to rule out someone totally until the guilty person was discovered. She'd been surprised a few times.

Brad and Mark were tailing the baby courier, who

was holed up in a shady hotel, not doing anything but, it seemed, waiting. For what? A payment? If so, who hired her? One of Jackson's men? Someone who could lead them to the middleman and ultimately Saunders? Or was Saunders Jackson?

Still nothing from Janice and Quinn about anyone connected to the moose lodge looking like the man who had turned out the lights. If they could find him, they might be able to locate Saunders, too.

And how does Hannah Adams fit into all of this? Does she? Just because she worked at a fertility clinic didn't automatically make her a suspect. That evening at the ball all she had done was share a dance with Saunders. He might be a weasel, but he was an attractive man if you liked the muscle-bound type.

The sound of the door opening halted her steps. She turned toward Tom Parks as he came into the office.

"I was told you wanted to see me." The thin, medium-size man hung back by the entrance as though he would flee at any moment. Worry carved deep lines into his youthful face. "Why does the FBI want to see me?"

Lisette gestured toward the second chair in front of the manager's desk. "Sit down. I have a few questions for you about the masquerade ball."

He looked at the seat warily. "I prefer to stand."

"You bumped into a guy dressed in a pirate's costume that evening. Did you give him anything?"

His jaw went slack. "I didn't do anything wrong."

"I didn't say you did. I was at the ball and noticed when you bumped into the pirate it appeared you slipped something into his pocket. What was it?"

She wasn't 100 percent sure, but she wasn't going to let

Tom know that. She stared him down until the guy averted his gaze and dropped his head.

"Someone paid me to give the man a note. That was all. I didn't see any harm in earning a generous tip."

"Just a piece of paper? Nothing else?"

"No. One small sheet folded and taped."

"Why did you bump into him? Why didn't you just hand it to the pirate?"

"He told me he didn't want anyone to know I was giving him a note. I'm not a pickpocket. I had to do something to get close to the man, so I acted like I'd tripped."

Lisette studied the waiter, whose direct stare didn't waver. "Is this the man who gave it to you?" She pulled out two pictures, one of the man with a moose logo on his coat and one of the bulky cohort with Saunders at the cabin that she'd worked with the sketch artist to draw.

Tom Parks tapped the man who had been with Saunders at the cabin. "That's him. He wasn't dressed in a costume. I thought he worked at the hotel."

"Why?"

"He came out a door for employees only."

"Have you ever seen him at the hotel other than that night?"

"No, but I'm pretty new so I don't know too many people working here."

"Thanks. I have your contact information from the manager if I need to talk to you again. Do you have any plans to go on vacation or leave town in the next few weeks?" They didn't have a few weeks to find Baby C.

"No. I'm trying to work as much as I can. Saving up for a car. That's why I jumped at the chance to fill in for a sick employee."

"How last minute was that?"

"The night manager called me frantic when one of his employees got sick and went home half an hour before the event was starting. I don't live far from the hotel."

"Remember, stay put in Denver." She walked to the door and opened it for Tom to exit. Out in the hall the manager was talking with an employee. She waited until he was finished, then showed him the two photos, which Colton was passing around to the security guards. "Do you know either one of these men?"

"Sure. He drives a delivery truck for McCartney Foods. He comes here about three times a week. At least, he did until recently. There's a new guy this week." The manager combed his fingers through his hair. "The staff really likes him. He's probably on vacation."

"What's his name?"

"Buddy Smith."

"May I have the name of your contact person and the phone number at McCartney Foods?" Lisette asked as Colton exited the elevator and strode toward her, his expression neutral.

"Let me get it." The manager slipped inside his office.

Colton stopped in front of Lisette. "I didn't get anything more from the security guys."

"I did. I know the name of the other man at the cabin with Saunders. Buddy Smith. He delivers food to the hotel. The manager is getting me the information of the supplier he works for."

"The more we investigate, the more people we find involved in some way with Saunders. I'm beginning to feel there is no middleman the deeper we investigate," Colton said, and then greeted the manager, who returned with the information Lisette requested.

"Thanks. I would appreciate it if you keep this to your-self." Lisette pulled out her cell phone.

"Not a word. I don't want our hotel known for being associated with a drug dealer."

While Lisette and Colton headed to the parking lot, she placed a call to the contact person at McCartney Foods. She finished talking with him, then slipped inside Colton's rental. "I've got an address for Buddy Smith. He took a week of his vacation, but you and I know he didn't leave town. Maybe we'll catch him at home."

"Wouldn't it be even better if Saunders was at Smith's house with Baby C?"

"We can wish. I suggest we get a warrant, and while we're waiting for that, we can case his house."

"Not an apartment?"

"The man I talked with said Smith lived in the fam-ily home."

"He's married, has a family?"

"No. His mother left it to him when she moved to Ari-zona. The guy at McCartney Foods said Smith was a great worker. Dependable. Rarely absent."

"He lives alone. That's good." Colton drove out of the hotel parking lot and turned toward the north part of Den-ver.

Lisette told Colton about the waiter giving Saunders a note. "I was beginning to think Saunders had written the note himself. Although I don't think Tom Parks, the waiter, is involved directly, I'm going to call my office and have an FBI agent tail him, especially since we don't know who slipped Saunders the tracking device."

"Someone did. What happened at the cabin is the re-sult of it. That person might not be one of the three we're looking into."

"Or it could be Hannah Adams."

"Yes." At a stop sign, Colton glanced at her. "We need to learn everything we can about her. After we have a talk with Buddy Smith."

Lisette's stomach rumbled.

Colton pulled into the intersection. "We'll stop and get something to eat. It may take a while to get a search warrant. If we have to be on a stakeout, we might as well have a late lunch."

"You'll get no argument from me. As you heard, I'm starved. I didn't eat the breakfast they brought to my room this morning. All I could think about was getting out of there. I hate hospitals."

"I feel that way, too. My mother died at a hospital, and I went into foster care after that. Did something happen for you to feel that way?"

Foster care. He'd said it casually, but looking at him, tension became evident in his grip on the steering wheel and the hard set to his jaws. "I'm sorry. I had a mother—" The partial sentence was out of her mouth before she could take it back.

He pulled into a fast food restaurant's drive-through. "I remember reading about your mother having to leave the FBI under questionable circumstances. That had to be hard on you."

She twisted toward him. "What have you heard?"

"You know how people like to gossip while hanging around waiting for something to happen."

"And you listen to gossip?" She couldn't keep the anger from infusing her voice.

"No." He stared at her. "I don't have time for that. But I can't always stop from hearing it. She didn't get charged with anything, so I figure she didn't do it or they couldn't prove it."

He didn't ask which was true. That was surprisingly refreshing. Most people did.

"What do you want to eat?"

"Hamburger, fries and coffee."

He placed their orders, getting the same thing as she did. When he inched his car toward the window, she expected him to say something, but he remained quiet. Relieved, she lounged back against the cushion, but the relaxation didn't last more than a few seconds. Respecting her privacy, he'd let the subject go. Another thing she liked about the man.

"Thank you."

He looked toward her. "For not prying? Partners don't do that to each other. You'll tell me if you want me to know. My asking you about your mother won't change that."

He pulled up, paid for the food, then took the bag it was in and handed it to Lisette.

The scent of grilled hamburger meat and French fries saturated every inch of the rental car. Lisette's stomach growled again.

Colton chuckled and eased into the stream of cars going north. "Let's go ahead and dig in while it's hot."

She tore into the sack, giving him his burger and fries first. Then she peeled off the wrapper and took a deep breath. As she chewed, she thought of what he'd said that had prompted her near-slip about her mother. "And anytime you want to talk about being in the foster care system, I'll listen."

"Why? Do you think there was a problem?"

"How old were you when your mother died?"

"Ten."

"Did you get adopted?"

"No. It can be hard...." His last word came out in a gruff whisper.

"I won't pry, either."

"So we'll sit in this car possibly for hours and twiddle our thumbs?"

"We can always discuss the weather."

"It's getting colder and clouds are starting to move in. There's a chance for snow. Not much to discuss."

"Do you think it will snow again?" Lisette peered at the sky turning darker.

"No, at least I'm hoping not. Okay, we exhausted that subject. What's next?"

"When are you leaving the Denver office?"

He popped a fry into his mouth. He didn't say anything while he changed lanes and put his blinker on to turn left. "Why did you ask that?"

"Your usual pattern is to stay for two years, then move on to another office. Your boss told me you had been in Denver two years."

"What else did he tell you?"

"You're a good marshal. You get your man. Those were his words, not mine."

"After this case is over, I'm going for interviews in Dallas and L.A."

"I can't help you with either place. Denver is the first sizable city I've been in."

"You graduated top of your class. You should have been able to pick where you went."

"That didn't happen." Before he asked why and they were back to the subject of her mother, Lisette asked, "Why do you like to move every two years? I hope I get to stay awhile in Denver. I like it."

"I like Denver, too, but I'm used to moving. I used to move a lot as a kid."

"The first eight years I lived in New Orleans, then we moved several times before ending up in the Washington, D.C., area. The stability of living in one place was nice in New Orleans. I call that place home."

He shrugged and parked a few houses down from Buddy Smith's. "I don't know anything else. I look at being assigned to a new place as an adventure."

"That kind of adventure I can do without. You have to learn who likes what or doesn't. There's always a pecking order at a new office."

"It's not a problem for me. When you don't care what others think about you, a heavy burden is lifted off you."

"So that's how you handle all those moves." She'd cared too much. That was why what happened after her mother's discharge had upset her so much. She was bothered about what people thought of her. Even if they never said anything directly to her, she knew they were judging her.

"If I hadn't, it would have made life difficult. I refuse to play those games. It was bad enough in school, but as an adult I wasn't going to."

"What's your secret?"

"I remember that in God's eyes we are equally loved, so I don't have to slave away trying to best another. He loves me for who I am."

The thought was freeing, but she couldn't convince herself to do that. She'd been measured against her mother all her life—first seeking her approval, and then later trying to live down her reputation.

"He loves you, too." Colton took the last bite of his hamburger, then washed it down with a gulp of coffee.

Did the Lord accept her with all her flaws? Her mother

never had been able to, and she was her parent. So how could she expect Him to?

"Make yourself comfortable. It may be a long afternoon." Colton adjusted his seat back from the steering wheel and relaxed. "At least it looks like someone is home. A car is in the driveway."

EIGHT

An hour later Colton hung up from talking to Quinn. "He's getting the search warrant and should be here soon."

"Did Janice come back with him or is she staying at the lodge?" Lisette leaned forward in the car and rolled her shoulders, then kneaded her nape.

"She'll check out the night shift and come back to Denver tomorrow morning unless we need her. So far they haven't discovered anyone who knows the light man, but they sell the coats in the gift shop at the lodge."

"Not that I haven't enjoyed sharing a few field stories—yours are much more interesting than mine—but I'm ready to pick up this Buddy Smith and find out what Saunders is planning. I hate the thought that Baby C. is being cared for by that man." Lisette shivered, hugging her arms.

"The sun might be back out now, but we're in the shade. You want me to turn the heat on?"

"It's not the cold so much as thinking about the child's life at stake, but I've got to admit it's getting chilly in here."

Colton reached to turn the key in the ignition. The past hour they'd exchanged information on the different jobs they had worked on, but they never went further into the past. It was as if they had silently agreed their childhoods were off-limits. He wanted it that way, but at the same time he wanted to know more about hers. He knew he couldn't have it both ways, but he felt a connection to her because of their childhoods. Although different, he sensed she'd been as lonely as he had.

"What if we've been here all this time and Smith isn't in the house?" Lisette put her hands up at a nearby vent to warm them.

"That might be the case, but even if he isn't there, we'll go in with the search warrant and see what we can find."

"I want the man. I have a score to settle. My head still throbs, and Neil won't be out of the hospital for another day."

Colton grinned, picturing Lisette trying to take down the man over six feet eight or so inches while she was no more than five-four. "If he's as big as you said, I want to see that."

"Do I detect amusement in your voice?"

He indicated an inch with his thumb and forefinger. "Just a little."

A movement at the front right window of Smith's house caught Colton's attention. "He's opening the blinds." He glimpsed a large shadow, then nothing. "Maybe he's getting up."

"Sleeping in. What is that?"

"Something we don't get when on a case."

"Let's get back to that amusement in your voice. I can take you down. It isn't size but technique."

"But size is an advantage."

She rolled her eyes. "Why do men—" She riveted her attention to the porch. "He's coming out."

Colton watched the massive man, probably three hundred pounds of muscles, lock his front door. Dressed in jeans, boots and a heavy overcoat with a backpack slung over his shoulder, Smith wasn't going to get his mail. "He's leaving. We'll apprehend him.

She looked at him. "Maybe we should follow him. He might take us to Saunders."

"We could, but we risk losing him in traffic. Rush hour has started. We have enough on him to pressure him into talking. Besides, we need to check his house. It's possible he has Baby C. Let's see if we can get nearer before he spots us."

"I'll exit out your side. It's closer to the curb and that hedge will block us some."

Colton eased his car door open and exited the vehicle while Lisette climbed over the console in the middle front seat and followed him to the sidewalk. After removing his gun from its holster, he stuck it in his pocket and kept his hand clutching it. "Right now he's in no hurry, but the second he really sees us and gets a good look, he'll make a run for his car. If we have to, shoot his tires while I approach him. We don't want him going anywhere or drawing a weapon."

He felt her presence behind him the whole time he was in front of Smith's neighbor's yard. When the huge man was ten or eleven feet from his car, he swung his backpack around and grasped it in his right hand.

With his Wilson Combat up and ready to shoot, Colton stepped out in clear view of Smith. "U.S. Marshal. Halt and get down on the ground."

Smith froze, his eyes growing big, his face going pale. Then suddenly he heaved his backpack at Colton, swung around and started running toward his house. Colton took out after him with Lisette right behind him. If he got inside, he could hole himself up in there. No telling what kind of firepower the man had in his place.

Pumping his legs as fast as he could go, Colton gained on the large man, the sound of his heavy breathing drifting to Colton.

Crack.

Smith went down on his steps. Colton dove for cover, using the porch as a shield. From the angle of the bullet hitting Smith, he had a little protection in his current position. He searched the terrain for a sign of where the sniper was while he shouted, "Lisette, okay?"

"Yeah, I'm behind the car. The shot came from that crop of trees in the yard next door."

Colton glanced at Smith and saw that his chest was rising and falling, but he'd been hit in the stomach and was bleeding heavily. He pulled out his cell and called for backup and an ambulance.

"I see movement," Lisette said in a whisper.

Colton stuffed his cell back in his pocket and turned his full attention to the grove of tall pines in the neighbor on the right's yard. A man in a dark hoodie made a move, sprinting away, using the cover of the trees.

"Help Smith. I'm going after the sniper. It might be Saunders. Similar in size and build."

With gun in hand, Colton sprinted across Smith's front yard and plunged into the small woods, using the pines as a shield. Adrenaline surged to every part of him, his heart racing.

The man, maybe a football field away, pivoted, planted himself behind a tree and took a shot.

Another shot rang out in the woods to the right. Lisette squinted in the glare of the sun off the white snow, trying to see Colton. She couldn't. She wanted to help Colton, but Smith was alive.

Lisette knelt down beside him, took off her coat and pressed it into his wound to try to stem the flow of blood. "An ambulance is on its way. Hang in there."

"He…betrayed me."

"Who? Saunders?"

"Yes." Smith coughed, blood trickling out of the corner of his mouth.

"Where is he? We can pick him up and make him pay for shooting you."

"House on…" More coughs racked Smith, bringing his head up off the step. He pointed down the street, then went limp and collapsed back onto the stair, his eyes staring at her.

A lifeless look.

The last shot had hit the tree inches from Colton, pieces of wood flying everywhere. Several stabbed him, stinging his cheek, arm and chest. He ducked back for a few seconds, then slowly peered around the trunk. The sniper was on the run again. Colton darted after him. His battered and bruised body caused by the wreck and shooting yesterday protested the punishing pace.

In some heavy brush, some evergreen, the man disappeared into the thicket. But Colton could hear the slapping of branches, the crunch of his steps in the icy snow. He followed the footsteps and the noise. The dense vegetation hindered his progress. A thorny bush snagged his coat. He slipped from it and kept going.

Suddenly he flew out into a clearing, stumbled and nearly fell into the snow. The only evidence someone had been there was the set of footprints that veered to the left and back into more undergrowth. The sound of an engine starting echoed through the quiet, followed by sirens coming closer. Colton raced in the direction of the car. He might still be able to stop the sniper.

Several yards ahead of him, he saw the back end of an old white Chevy. As it went around a bend, he glimpsed the first three numbers of a Missouri license plate—171.

Colton leaned over, dragging in deep breaths of the frigid air. Straightening, he called Lisette to warn her in case the sniper went back to see if Smith was still alive.

"He got away in a white Chevy ten years old with a partial license number—171. He might want to finish the job."

"It's too late. Smith died. The ambulance is here and a sheriff's car is pulling up."

"Let them know about the car and put a BOLO out on it. The driver is over six feet tall, probably about two hundred pounds. It could be Saunders but I'm not sure. I'll be back in a few minutes."

"You okay? You sound out of breath."

"I am. I've lived here two years and still get winded at this altitude."

"We have a lead from Smith so hurry."

Lisette picked up Smith's backpack and checked the contents—a gun and ammunition along with some money and a change of clothes. No directions to Saunders's location or a map with a big *X* to mark the spot where he was with Baby C. Smith just couldn't have made it easy for them.

Using Smith's set of keys from his pocket, Lisette let herself into the house and did a walk through to make sure Baby C wasn't inside. She found nothing to even indicate a child had been in the house at one time. She went back outside and covered the distance to Smith's car, checking the trunk and the inside of the vehicle. Again nothing. She sensed Colton before she saw him coming out of the small grove of trees, slipping into his overcoat.

She met him halfway across the yard. "I went through Smith's backpack and briefly checked his house and car for signs of Baby C. I didn't find anything of use. I think we should canvas the area as soon as possible. At the end, Smith said, 'House on…' and pointed toward the west like he was indicating a place where Saunders was. It may be on this street. If not, we should expand our search. He could have been nearby. Since his neighborhood has large pieces of property with lots of trees, it isolates each home from the others. A good place to hide."

"Agreed. I'm calling in help with the surrounding streets while we take this one. I'm sure Saunders is long gone if that was him, but we might find a clue to where he's going or who he's contacting to sell the baby to. He would have left in a hurry, if Saunders is the sniper and in a nearby house. That could lead to a mistake."

"Want to split up?"

"It's probably better not to. The man is desperate."

Lisette gestured at the west end of the block. "We should start there."

"Just a sec. I need to call my boss. I'll have him organize the search of the other streets. He should be here soon. I'll have Quinn go through Smith's place."

"I'll let the two deputies secure Smith's house." Lisette made her way to the nearest one. "Marshal Phillips and I are canvassing the street. Guard the house. Don't let anyone inside until Marshal Parker shows up."

Two minutes later she and Colton walked toward the end of the block. He'd gotten an extra coat from his car for her since hers was bloodied. When they approached a one-story tan house with peeling paint and a broken porch swing, Colton rang the bell.

"Yes, can I help you?" An elderly sounding voice came through the still-closed door.

"Ma'am, I'm Deputy U.S. Marshal Phillips, and the woman with me is Special Agent Sutton with the FBI. There was a shooting down the street, and we would like to have a word with you."

The door opened a few inches with a chain still on it. A gray-haired lady with a sweater on asked, "Let me see your credentials."

Colton showed her his and then Lisette did the same. Stepping back, Colton waved for her to talk to the woman. Lisette moved forward while her partner kept an eye on the area.

"Do you know Buddy Smith, who lives across the street three houses down from you?"

"I knew his mom. Don't have much reason to know him. He used to give his ma problems. Is he the one who was shot?"

"Yes. May we come in and talk?"

"No way, José. I don't open the door for any stranger."

"Okay. I can understand that. Have you noticed anything unusual going on here the past few days?"

"Quiet until today. I nearly had a heart attack when I heard the gunshots. More than one. Scary." The woman frowned.

"What's your name?"

"Mabel Vance. Been living here for forty years."

"So other than this afternoon, there's been nothing out of the ordinary occurring on this street?"

"I didn't say that. I said it has been quiet."

"So something unusual did happen?" Lisette glanced back at Colton.

"Yes, next door. I heard a baby crying at night for hours. The house is rented, but I ain't heard a baby crying there in years."

Lisette looked toward the piece of property Mabel was talking about. The homes were fifty feet apart, closer than most on the block, but still far away if the windows were shut to hear a child screaming. And since it was winter, Lisette doubted either had opened the windows. "You've got exceptional hearing."

"Not really. I was outside taking my garbage out. The can is on that side of the house. The crying was faint, but I'm sure it was a baby. No TV because it went on and on. No person in their right mind would watch a show that long with that racket."

"Did you ever see the person who rented the house?"

"A woman a week ago but I haven't seen her since. She had a cute yellow bug."

"A Volkswagen?"

"Yes."

"There wasn't a man with her?"

"Not that I saw. I keep an eye on the neighborhood, but even I have to sleep."

Colton descended the steps to the sidewalk, studying the white brick house next door.

Lisette poked a card through the small opening. "Call me if you think of anything else. Thanks, Mabel. You've been a big help." She started to turn away and stopped. "Oh, Mabel, what did the woman look like?"

"A looker. Dark hair, curvy body. Probably broke a lot of men's hearts."

"How tall?"

"Don't rightly know that. Average, I guess."

"How old would you guess her to be?"

"Twenties. Thirties."

"Who's the landlord?"

"He lives on the other side. Ron Perkins."

"Thanks again." Lisette hurried to catch up with Colton, who plodded across the yard in the snow toward the house in question. "The lady she described could be Hannah Adams, except for the color of the hair. She's blonde."

"That could be a wig." Colton mounted the couple of steps to the front door and knocked since there was no doorbell.

Lisette went to the window, but the blinds were closed and there was no way to look inside. "Let's go ask the landlord to let us in."

"You go ahead. I'll stay out here and watch the house and neighborhood."

At Mr. Perkins's, she quickly explained their need, and he grabbed his keys and went back with her.

"A nice lady rented the house for the month. Paid me cash. She had a friend coming to spend some time in Denver."

"Who was she?"

"Harriet Peabody. She showed me a driver's license."

"Did you take down her license number and address?"

"Sure did. I've got it back at my place."

When Lisette ascended to the porch, Colton extended a gloved hand and opened the door. "I tried it and it wasn't locked. Do I have permission to enter your rental?"

Mr. Perkins nodded.

Lisette turned to the landlord. "Would you please go get me the information you have on Harriet Peabody?"

The bald man grinned. "Sure. I always like to help the police or, in your case, the FBI. I'll be right back."

Lisette decided to stay on the porch until he returned so Mr. Perkins wouldn't come inside. Her instinct told her Harriet Peabody was Hannah Adams. Maybe something in the house would confirm that. She felt they were getting closer to Saunders, but would they be too late to keep Baby C from being sold?

Colton would first do a walk-through to see if he could find anything to indicate that Saunders had been staying here, especially with Baby C, or evidence of who this Harriet Peabody was. Hannah Adams? There were similarities in the description of the two women. Stepping into the second bedroom in the house, he scanned it, not seeing anything that caught his eye except there was a drawer missing in a dresser. He moved around the twin bed to get a better look and nearly stumbled over the drawer on the floor with a blanket lining its bottom.

Where Baby C slept?

Possibly. But he didn't want to jump to conclusions just because he wanted it to be that way. That would probably mean the man who shot Buddy Smith was Saunders and he'd made a run for it with Baby C. With a description of the car he was driving, the police might be able to track it down. He prayed that was the case because each day they didn't find the child the chances grew that she'd become lost to them.

"Did you find anything?" Lisette said from the doorway.

"Possibly where Baby C slept. I'll call in the crime scene techs and hopefully they'll be able to pull Saunders's fingerprints from here. Maybe the woman's, too."

"If she's in the database. Saunders is, but she might not be. We already checked on Hannah Adams and she isn't. We need a set of her fingerprints to compare to the ones we find here."

"My gut is telling me she's involved somehow with Saunders. But if Harriet Peabody isn't Hannah Adams, then at least when we find the woman who rented this house, we'll have evidence to support our case against her."

Lisette moved farther into the room, rounding the bed and staring at the drawer on the floor. "I've got the information from the landlord about Harriet Peabody. I'm having one of the FBI agents at the office run it for me. If Saunders was the one here, I'm sure the info is bogus. I showed Mr. Perkins the picture we had from the hotel camera of Little Bo Peep—Hannah Adams. It wasn't clear, but he thought it could be Harriet Peabody in a blond wig. I'll bring back a better picture later and see if he can ID her positively."

"So now we have to wait."

"We still have Hannah Adams to interview."

"I'd like to wait until after we get the evidence back from this house. If Hannah Adams is involved, the best way we might discover what's happening at the clinic is to have you go in undercover. I don't want to tip her off that we suspect her."

"As a client or employee?" Lisette adjusted her glasses and glanced around the bedroom.

"The more we investigate, the more I think you need to get a job at the clinic. Marshal Benson has been monitoring the activities of the clinic, and he told me this morning they have an agreement with a nursing agency for temporary help when needed. He's contacted the owner and can put you in as a nurses' aide. From what I understand, your duties would be mostly following the orders of the nurse or doctor at the clinic. Setting up for patients, cleaning up after they leave, taking information down. They have someone going on vacation in a couple of days."

"In two days?" She sighed. "I've had first aid training. I'm sure I can take a crash course on what would be expected of me as a nurses' aide. I think I need to do that."

"I think so, too. You really only have one day since we'll probably be tied up today. I'll ask Marshal Benson to set someone up for tomorrow to help you." Colton pulled out his cell phone and arranged to have a crime scene unit go through the house for evidence. "Let's finish our walk-through, then go back to Smith's and see what Quinn has discovered."

When Colton turned toward the hallway, he spied a trash can partially behind the door. He strolled to it. "Dirty diapers are in here. Small ones." He looked toward Lisette. "We're getting close."

She nodded. "I can't wait to bring that man down."

Colton followed her into the hallway and strode toward the last bedroom, making a survey of the room. Nothing. "I've still got the kitchen, then we'll leave."

When he arrived in the kitchen, he stopped in the middle, noting the food out on the counter and a pan on the stove. He walked to it and peered into it. "Soup." Gesturing toward the can nearby, he added, "Chicken noodle. Another half an inch and it would have been gone in the pot," then reached to turn the burner off.

"I did that once with some water I was boiling. Forgot all about it until a burning smell reminded me. It scorched my stovetop." Lisette opened the refrigerator. "Two baby bottles in here. He must have really made a fast getaway if he didn't take these."

"And that could lead to mistakes." Colton started for the front of the house. "We've done what we can until forensics has been run on this place."

Outside again, Colton breathed in a deep gulp of air as though that would cleanse him of the dirty feeling he had after going through the house. Selling babies was about as low a person could go in his book.

Lisette paused next to him, her eyes closed.

"You felt it, too. The evil in that place."

"Yes. The only consolation is that he will keep Baby C alive because she is important to him. I've been involved in several kidnappings where that wasn't the case. One child was killed. That broke my heart. I had a difficult time recovering from it. I was so angry at the Lord for letting that happened."

"He isn't the one who kidnapped the baby. A person was. Bad things happen to good people. In this life there is no Garden of Eden."

"But you console yourself with the fact that justice will prevail in the end. If not in this life, the everlasting one. Where were you when I was struggling with that?"

Facing her, he clasped her hand, something he would normally consider unprofessional and something he wouldn't do, but the pain dripping off Lisette's words made the gesture feel right. "My outlook took years to form. I used to get angry like you. I'd rail at God. Then I read a passage in the Bible where it says, 'Vengeance is mine,' and it began to fall into place for me."

One corner of her mouth lifted. "Now if I could just work on forgiving, life might be a little easier."

"I'm working on that one, too." He released her hand and began walking toward Smith's house. "When we have time, you can tell me about yours and I'll tell you about mine." That sentence slipped out before he realized what it would mean to him. He wanted to take it back, but maybe he said it because he did need to share with a person he respected and cared about.

She didn't say anything. Instead, she increased her pace as though needing to put some space between them. It had to be her mother. She'd shut down the last time she'd been close to saying something about her mother.

Colton opened the front door to Smith's house, and Lisette proceeded inside. The crime scene techs were processing the living room. Quinn saw them and crossed to them.

"So far nothing to give us a lead to Saunders. But Smith had a book with phone numbers and access codes to websites on the internet. One of the entries for a phone number was listed under D.S. on the last page. I'm figuring that's Don Saunders."

"Did you try the phone number?"

Quinn smiled. "Yep, and a man answered. I'm positive it was Saunders. He hurriedly hung up, and when I called back, it rang until a recording picked up. I want to leave and see if I can track anything on Saunders's phone number."

"It's probably an untraceable cell number, but we need to run it down. Lisette and I will stay. Another team is coming to process the house near the end of the block. I think Saunders was staying there, and he was the guy that shot Smith."

"I'll call you if I discover anything useful."

"Let me know when you rule it out as a lead."

"Sure." Quinn left the house.

As the door clicked shut, Colton's cell phone rang. He noticed it was the sheriff's office. "Marshal Phillips."

"This is Sheriff Dailey here. We found the white car you identified leaving the scene of the crime." The sheriff went on to describe where the Chevy was in a rural area just south of Denver.

"Did you get anything from the vehicle?"

"No. It was set on fire, out in the middle of nowhere."

"Fan out and search the area. I'm sending you a picture of the man I think was in the car. He may be on foot with a kidnapped baby. I'll be right there." He disconnected with the sheriff, caught Lisette staring at him and continued, "He's making mistakes. He's harried and not thinking things through. I hope this doesn't cause an innocent baby to be hurt."

NINE

Lisette stared out her side window in the car at the scene of the abandoned Chevy in the field. The charred remains of the car disturbed the pristine white of the snow—that and myriad footprints marred it. Three law enforcement officers were at the scene with the one in the center probably the sheriff.

After buttoning her heavy coat, Lisette put on her gloves. "I hope they know which tracks are Saunders's. Having snow can be a good thing unless the path has been destroyed."

As another sheriff's car arrived and parked behind Colton, he opened his door. "I'd hoped they were already searching the area nearby."

"It might be a man power problem."

"That's why I called the state police to aid us, as well."

Lisette paused next to the Jeep. "From what I see, all footprints lead back to the road. I can't see any going away from the car in any other directions. So why did he drive off here—" she pointed at the set of tire tracks going down the gentle slope to the pasture "—through the fence and into the field?"

"And why set the car on fire? To cover any forensic evidence?"

"We don't know for sure the sniper is Saunders so that might be why. The person in the house left in a hurry, leaving his food cooking on the stove, so I guess trying to cover up any evidence might be why, but it calls attention to the car immediately."

Lisette traversed the incline, following in Colton's steps next to the tire tracks in the snow. "The sniper might be someone different than who was at the house. It looks like someone walked in these tracks."

"Easier than plowing through a foot of snow."

A slamming car door drew Lisette's attention. A medium-height man held the leash of a bloodhound. "Looks like we've got some help."

"Good. There are a lot of questions. Few answers." Colton shook hands with the sheriff when he had finished giving instructions to his deputies.

Sheriff Dailey greeted Lisette with a nod. "There is one set of footprints leaving the car. The driver walked back there—" he pointed toward the road "—using the tracks he made in the snow. I called Al to bring Boomer, but I suspect the driver either got a ride with someone or he was picked up by an associate."

"That's a definite possibility. Saunders has people helping him."

Al with his bloodhound joined them. "What's up?"

The sheriff bent over and petted the dog. "We need to see where the driver went after leaving the car. If he hiked somewhere, we need to know that. It's hard to tell on the road. My deputy pulled up and what footprints were there were run over."

"Boomer, let's get to work. The faster we find the driver, the faster we get to warm back up."

Colton stepped forward. "I'm Marshal Phillips, and we

believe this is an escaped criminal. This is Agent Sutton of the FBI. We appreciate you coming out on this cold day."

"I heard a child was involved. I'd come out in a blizzard if I had to." Al squatted and whispered something to Boomer, then when he stood, the bloodhound took off with his handler trailing after him.

Colton followed with the sheriff while Lisette stayed back a moment to examine the car. "It looks like he set the seat on fire and it spread from there."

"Yes, ma'am. That's what I figured, too." The deputy glanced at the dog and his handler. "I'm sorry I drove over the footprints up on the road. At the time I was responding to a call about the fire from the dispatcher, and I wanted to see if anyone had managed to get out of the car and was hurt."

"Who reported the car on fire?"

"The dispatcher didn't know."

"Male or female?"

"Female."

"And you didn't see anyone on the road as you drove here?"

"Nope. I came from the north so they must have headed south."

"Thanks." Lisette strolled around the car. What kind of game was Saunders playing? Was he even in the car? Was the woman Harriet Peabody in it?

"Lisette," Colton called out. "The trail leads this way." He waved his hand south.

Lisette hustled toward the road, the movement warming her body, but the wind cut through the layers of clothing to chill her when she crested the incline. On the pavement she hurried and caught up with Colton. "So he walked for a while."

"It looks that way."

The sheriff's cell rang, and he answered it. "Yep. I know where that is. We're not far." He turned toward Colton and Lisette. "A man was found on the side of the road about a mile down thataway." He pointed south.

"Is he dead?" Lisette asked, wondering if it was Saunders.

"Nope but unconscious. The lady who found the man called 9-1-1 for an ambulance."

"What lady?" Colton started walking again to keep up with Al and Boomer.

"Don't know. She didn't leave a name, and her number couldn't be traced." Sheriff Dailey sprinted after Al.

"A lady called in the fire on the car," Lisette said, throwing a glance toward the field before they went around a bend in the road and lost sight of the charred car.

"Someone with Saunders? That's possible. The footprints were messed up as if Saunders or someone purposely made them wide."

"I wonder what Hannah Adams is doing right now?"

"Great idea. We should see if we can find her. Keep an eye on her. She's the only woman besides the courier we know is involved, and since the courier is being tailed, it probably isn't her." He removed one glove and placed a call to Marshal Benson. After filling him in on what was happening at the car, Colton continued, "See if Hannah Adams can be found and watched. She should be at work." When he hung up, he smiled at Lisette. "Maybe you won't have to cram tomorrow for the nurses' aide job."

"I'm fine with that. I have to say I hate being reminded of school."

Colton's eyebrow rose. "You waited until the last minute to cram for a test?"

"Yes."

"I never took you for that. You're so thorough in your job."

"And you?"

"No, I always studied ahead of time so I relaxed the day before the test."

She chuckled. "I didn't take you for that."

"So we both have surprises."

Boomer stopped ten yards up the road and sat. Al pivoted toward them and said, "The trail ends here."

The sheriff glanced around. "I don't see a man."

Colton reached him. "Maybe this is where someone picked up our suspect. It doesn't feel like we've gone a mile. He could have incapacitated the driver up the road, around that curve, then stolen his car."

"We'll keep going a little longer and see if Boomer picks up anything," the sheriff said to Al.

Lisette looked at the western sky with streaks of pink and orange cutting through the blue. "The sun is going down."

The sheriff made a call and asked one of his deputies to drive this way. "Yes, and if you think this is cold, wait till it gets dark."

Boomer disappeared around the bend in the road. A few seconds later, barking echoed through the quiet. Colton set out in a jog with Lisette, passing the sheriff. Her hand went to her holster at her waist at the same time Colton clasped the handle of his gun.

Rounding the curve, she spied Al kneeling by a body in the snow while the sound of sirens filled the air.

The sheriff came up behind them. "Thankfully our dispatcher called an ambulance earlier."

Al peered over his shoulder. "He's breathing but unre-

sponsive. It looks like he was dumped and rolled to here."
The dog handler rose and gestured at the snow nearby.

"So it's possible a woman may be with the driver of
the white car and there were two people and a baby in the
car," Colton said to the sheriff, noting that the unconscious
man wasn't Saunders.

At that moment Colton's cell phone rang. He looked at
the caller screen and answered. "We found the man we
think picked up whoever was in the white Chevy. He was
left unconscious by the roadside. Were you able to locate
Hannah?"

As Colton listened, a frown deepened the lines on his
face. By the time he hung up, he was scowling. "Hannah
can't be found. She took today off from work. Her car is
in the driveway of her duplex, but she isn't at home. My
boss is leaving someone at her place. He'll let me know
when she comes back home."

The ambulance pulled up, and two paramedics began
tending to the man who appeared to be about seventy. The
deputy parked behind where Lisette and Colton watched
them work on the victim.

In the midst of the activity, the sheriff received another
call, then strode to them. "Benjamin Mason reported someone stole his car. He lives four miles south of this location."

Colton swung his gaze to her. "We'll need to check
this out. Until this man wakes up, we won't know what
happened."

Lisette shook her head. "I feel like we're in a three-ring
circus with the clowns running it."

"It does seem like Saunders is having fun leading us
on a wild-goose chase." Colton turned back to the sheriff.
"Do you know who the victim is?"

"Nope. Not from around here, but the paramedics gave

me his billfold. The man is Keith Olson from Boulder. I'll run his driver's license and see what kind of car he was driving, then put an alert out on it."

"Good. Agent Sutton and I will check out the stolen car while you coordinate the search for this man's car. I'll call you with what we find."

Darkness blanketed the landscape as Colton and Lisette approached a farmhouse where the owner reported his car stolen. No lights were on in the house.

Colton switched off the engine but left his headlights on since only a half-moon illuminated the area. "We're being given the runaround. We didn't see any abandoned cars on the way here. No sign of the Cougar." While driving to the ranch, the sheriff had called to let them know Keith Olson drove a Cougar. "So why would Saunders steal another vehicle if nothing was wrong with the one he was driving?"

"Good question. Maybe he realized the other car could be identified. But with Saunders, who knows."

"You know, I've got a feeling he's setting us up."

"A trap? I can see that."

"But we still need to check this out. There could be someone else hurt inside."

"I'll go around the house while you knock on the front door. Maybe there's a light on in the back, but we can't see it from the drive."

The hairs on his nape stood up. He didn't have a good feeling about this. Saunders didn't care who was in his way. The man unconscious at the side road was at least seventy years old. Colton climbed out of the Jeep and removed his gun from its holster. "Circle the house, then come back to the porch."

He couldn't see a bell, so he swung the screen door

open and knocked. The loud noise sounded, alerting any-one close by, but he wanted to make sure the owner heard him because what he was going to do next wasn't by the book. He didn't want to take a chance in case the owner was hurt—because why wouldn't he be here if he called 9-1-1 for help? His gut twisted with all the possibilities running through his mind.

He hated this feeling of walking into a trap but having no choice. He tried the door but it was locked. He knelt and picked the lock, using his penlight to illuminate the area. Adrenaline pumped through his body, every sense alert. With his weapon in his hand, he eased the door open. In-side, a light glowed from the rear of the house.

Behind him, Lisette entered. "Someone is on the floor in the kitchen."

Colton pulled the string on the lamp nearby. "I'll take that part of the house while you check the other." He waved to the right and began moving that way toward the kitchen.

As he made his way through the living room and din-ing room, he shouted, "Clear."

Lisette did the same.

In the kitchen, Colton knelt next to the man on the floor, blood on the back of his head, and felt his pulse at his neck.

"Is he alive?" Lisette asked behind him.

"No. He's been hit," he said, surveying the area, "prob-ably by that." He indicated a meat tenderizer lying on the floor a few feet from the victim.

Colton rose. "He called 9-1-1 about his car being stolen, and then he was hit? What is going on here?" He shook his head. "I'm calling this in, then we need to check the barn. I don't see a garage so maybe he kept his vehicle in the barn."

He placed a call to the sheriff and told him what happened.

"Benjamin Mason was a grumpy old man, but I don't know anyone who had a beef with him. He has a brandnew red Ford 150. He was so proud of that truck. He didn't even have a license plate for it yet." The sheriff's heavy sigh sounded through the connection. "I'll get an alert out for the truck."

"There's no sign of Keith Olson's Cougar, but we'll take a look in the barn."

"I'll have a couple of deputies there ASAP. We'll concentrate our search around there. See if anyone has seen the truck. It seems like the person you're after is going south toward Denver so I'll let the police there know."

Something nagged Colton. He hung up and started for the front door. "Let's check the barn. The snow should give us an indication of what happened. I'm getting some flashlights from the Jeep."

"If I was running from the police, I wouldn't be leaving a trail for them to follow." Lisette walked beside him to the car.

"I wouldn't, either." He kneaded his nape. "Something else is going on here."

"A diversion?"

"Maybe. I wish we had more man power, but some of it is needed other places."

"Which Saunders may be using to his advantage."

Colton handed a heavy-duty flashlight to Lisette, then trudged through the foot-deep snow toward the barn on the left side of the house about a hundred yards away. Sweeping his light over the area in front of him, he frowned. "Lots of footprints. Different sizes and types of shoes. Here's one that is made by cowboy boots. This one is a sneaker and over there a boot. We have no idea which ones are the old man's."

"He had on house slippers in the kitchen so that doesn't help. We can check his closet later."

"No fresh tire tracks. Interesting."

Fifty feet from the barn, the double doors busted open and a red truck barreled straight for them. The headlights blinded Colton. He lifted his gun, started to shoot, but stopped when he thought of Baby C possibly in the vehicle. Diving out of the way at the last second, he twisted at the same time and got a glimpse of the driver and the shadow of a person in the passenger's seat. The engine revved as the Ford sped away, its rear swinging from side to side.

Colton popped up off the ground. "Lisette, are you okay?" he asked as he aimed and squeezed off a shot, the bullet hitting the ground near the back tire.

"What if that's Saunders, and Baby C is in there?"

He slanted a look toward her while picking up the flashlight he'd dropped. "I want to let them know I'm serious, but I didn't shoot close on purpose. Saunders isn't driving. Something else is happening here."

Wincing, she rose slowly.

"Are you sure you're okay?"

Lisette rubbed her left arm. "Yes, I just fell wrong. I'll be able to shake it off. Let's go after whoever they are."

Colton jogged toward his Jeep, and as he started the car, Lisette hopped into the passenger seat. He threw the rental into four-wheel drive and charged down the road after the driver in the truck. Bouncing over ruts, he gripped the steering wheel as tight as he could. He took the turn onto the highway, pressing down on the gas as much as he could afford. The back of the Jeep fishtailed, but he righted it and pursued the stolen vehicle.

"Sheriff, this is Agent Sutton. We're following a red Ford 150 south on the highway from Mason's ranch. There are two people in the cab of the truck. Our speed is nearing sixty miles an hour." Lisette paused, as though listening. "Yes. I appreciate that."

Colton tossed her a glance, then quickly returned his full attention to the chase. When she disconnected the call, he asked, "What's he doing?"

"Setting up a roadblock. They should have one in place another ten miles or so. He said there are no highway turnoffs."

"Good. Maybe we'll catch these two."

"Are they part of Saunders's gang?"

"Maybe. Either way I won't let these guys get away. They killed an old man for a truck."

"With all that Saunders has done lately, this doesn't feel right. The man I got to know would be long gone the first chance he got. It's possible Saunders wasn't in the white car when it went off the road, but he's behind this. If we catch these guys, we might find out something to help us."

Colton kept right up with the truck, determined to drive them toward the roadblock. Just a few more miles and they would have the suspects. "I'm beginning to think it was a total setup from the start. Why set a getaway car on fire? Yes, I know it can cover up fingerprints and other evidence, but the car was in plain view from the road."

He pressed down on the accelerator, increasing his speed ten more miles an hour to keep pace with the truck in front of him, but with the snow-packed pavement anything could send his car off the road. *Lord, I need You to keep us safe. I have to find Baby C and Saunders and bring him to justice.*

Through the darkness of night Colton spied the headlights of the vehicles used in the roadblock. "I hope these guys don't try to run it."

Suddenly at the last second, the driver in the truck swerved to the right, going off-road into a field. Colton followed. The Ford 150 hit a snowbank and came to a stop. The doors to the truck opened, and two figures piled out of it into the cold night.

"The snow is too deep to drive any farther. We'll have to chase them on foot." Colton stopped, noticing behind him more police cars were coming out into the pasture.

Lisette drew her gun and climbed from the Jeep at the same time Colton did. "The good news is they'll have to plow through the snow first. We just have to follow them. Less work."

"My body thanks them for that." Colton joined her on the passenger's side nearer to the truck.

Moving as fast as he could, Colton reached the Ford 150 and found their trail. In the glow from the headlights, he zeroed in on the two suspects trudging through foot-high snow toward the tree line. Only yards away.

"U.S. Marshal. Stop or I'll fire," Colton yelled.

The pair kept going. Colton raised his gun and fired into the ground near him. The suspects fell, trying to bury themselves in the snow.

"I'm glad they didn't know I wouldn't shoot them unless armed, and I don't see a gun," Colton said, hurrying toward the two on the ground, now cowering at his approach.

He removed his handcuffs and locked them around one assailant's wrist while Lisette took care of the other, then he rolled over his man—probably in his early twenties.

"This one can't be over eighteen," Lisette said as she yanked on him to stand.

"I'm twenty, lady." The one with blond hair scowled at Lisette.

"Who are you?"

His eyes narrowed, and he clamped his mouth shut.

Lisette patted him down and found his wallet. Flipping it open, she found his driver's license. "Jordan Jones, you're in a lot of trouble." She tugged on his arm and started for the sheriff's four-wheel-drive SUV.

Colton towered over his assailant—on the small side but with piercing hard eyes aimed at Colton. He reached down and took hold of the guy and hauled him to his feet, then checked him for any weapons and his ID. When he pulled the young man's wallet from his back pocket, he started toward the sheriff. "You may not see the light of day for a long time for what you did today. Robbery, assault and murder, not to mention endangering police officers, me for one, with your reckless driving."

"Murder? I ain't kilt nobody. That old man by the road was alive when we left him."

Lisette sat across from twenty-five-year-old Harrison Giles, his expression frozen in a scowl since the deputy had brought him into the interrogation room five minutes ago. "This is your opportunity to make a deal. Your crimes are serious. You may think it was fun driving all over the county joyriding, but you tossed an old man out of his car when he'd stopped to help you. Keith Olson is in the hospital and is conscious. He's identified you and your friend out of a photo array."

"He was a fool to stop like that." Harrison studied his fingernails.

"From what the deputy at the hospital told me, you two

made it nearly impossible for him to do anything else. You took a risk lying down on the road."

Harrison shrugged. "Life's a risk."

"I'm glad you think that." Lisette ground her teeth to calm herself before proceeding with the interview. Losing control wouldn't help her. She bottled up her anger and contempt and narrowed her gaze on Harrison. "Then you and your buddy murdered Benjamin Mason and stole his truck. We have you fleeing the scene of the crime."

"Who? Don't know him? We took a truck, but we ain't kilt this guy, and ya can't frame us for it."

"My partner is talking with your buddy. The first one to talk will get a deal. If you want to play it that way, then you'll be going away for life. Good thing you like to take risks. Prison will be a continuous risk. You should enjoy that." Lisette scooted her chair back, surged to her feet and opened the door. "Deputy, he's ready to go back to his cell."

"Wait!" Harrison's voice held a touch of panic.

She pivoted in the entrance, her arms crossed over her chest.

"I'm tellin' the truth. I ain't a murderer."

"That isn't good enough. The evidence says you are."

Fear leaked into the man's face. "What evidence? I never saw this guy at the ranch."

"When you decide to tell the truth, I'll listen."

She started down the hallway toward the sheriff's office with Harrison yelling, "I ain't a murderer." Glancing back at the deputy at the door, she said, "Let him cool off in his cell. Get a taste of what prison will be like." Then she slipped into the room where the interviews were being taped to see what Colton was finding out from Jordan Jones, the blond-headed partner.

Wide-eyed, Jordan stared at Colton. "I'm not lying. I didn't kill anybody."

"Benjamin Mason called the police and reported someone stole his truck. When my partner and I came to investigate, we found him dead in the kitchen. He'd been hit over the head, but I don't know if that was the cause of death. The autopsy will be able to tell us that." Colton slid a photo of the crime scene across the table.

Jordan's face went pale, his hands shaking so much he clasped them together on the table. "We never saw him. We were told about the new truck."

Lisette sat up straight in her chair. *We were told?* Both she and Colton had thought there was something fishy about what had happened after the sniper drove off in the white Chevy.

"What do you mean? Told by who?" Colton asked, drawing her attention to the monitor.

"That lady who paid us."

"What lady?" Lisette said out loud, itching to be in the room with Colton.

"Paid you to do what?" Colton leaned across the table.

Lisette couldn't see his expression, but from the sound of his voice it had to be intense.

"I don't know her name but she gave us two hundred dollars to stop a car on the road, take it and then go to the ranch. She told us there was a brand-new Ford 150 in the barn. We were to steal it, and if we wanted to sell it after we did, she'd tell us where to take it. She told us to drive around until then. We would get to keep the cash from the sale, plus a thousand dollars more." The explanation flowed rapidly from Jordan as he twisted his hands together.

"Where's the Cougar you stole first?"

"There's a turnoff before getting to the ranch house. We hid it in the trees."

"Who were you going to sell the truck to?"

"Don't know. She was going to call us this evening by eight."

"How?"

"On Harrison's cell."

Colton glanced at his watch. "She's late. It's after nine."

Tears filled Jordan's eyes. "It was supposed to be fun. Easy cash."

"Can you describe her?"

Jordan shook his head. "Never saw her. Harrison made the arrangements with her."

Colton rose and walked toward the door.

"Where are you going?" Jordan yanked at the handcuffs around his wrists. "What am I supposed to do?"

"Stay and think about what you did. The man you left at the side of the road has a severe concussion."

Lisette left the viewing room and met Colton in the hallway. "Harrison is back in his cell. I think that would be a good place to show him Hannah's picture. The bars might jiggle his mind."

"Not cooperating?"

"No, but at least neither one has asked for his lawyer yet, although they were read their rights."

Colton accompanied Lisette to the set of cells the sheriff had at his station.

She took the photo of Hannah Adams and plastered it against the bars. "Is this the woman who hired you to steal two vehicles?"

Sitting on his bunk, Harrison looked up and frowned. "Jordan talked?"

"Yes. Is this the woman who paid you? If you didn't

murder Benjamin Mason, most likely she did. Do you want to go to prison for something she did?"

Harrison blinked his eyes open wide and pushed off his bed. At the bars, he took hold of the photo and pulled it toward him. He squinted. His forehead wrinkled. "I can't tell for sure. The lady I met with had bright red hair, big glasses and a mole on her upper lip. This lady doesn't, so I guess not."

"But the photo looks somewhat familiar?"

"Yeah, I guess. Maybe." He stuffed it through the bars.

Lisette grabbed it as the man sauntered to his bunk and sat again. "I understand she was supposed to call you with a place to sell the truck and give you the rest of the money. Did she?"

"Nope. I thought the money was too good to be true."

"Where did you meet her?"

"At Joe's Bar two days ago she'd come up to me and said she'd heard I needed money. I said yeah. I ain't gonna turn down easy money. I have debts. She'd call me when she needed me and said I could make thousands of dollars."

"I asked her who I had to kill. She laughed and said nothing like that. She even gave me two hundred dollars to be available at a moment's notice."

"Did she tell you who she was?"

"Yeah. Harriet Peabody."

Lisette peered at Colton standing off to the side. "How were you going to get the thousand dollars?"

"When she called with the information about which car shop to take the truck to, she would arrange a place to meet me." Harrison scanned the small cell. "I guess she played me for a fool." He stretched out on the bed and rolled toward the wall.

Lisette had no sympathy for the duo. They hadn't

thought a second about the man on the side of the road. They had given her and Colton a merry chase.

After telling the sheriff where the Cougar was, Lisette accompanied Colton from the station, exhausted but in no way ready to go to bed.

She'd clutched the door handle on Colton's Jeep so hard, she broke a couple of fingernails. "I don't know about you, but I'm starved and tired. This has been one long day."

"Let's go to Maxie's, then I'll take you home." He ran his gaze over her face.

Leaving a warm trail where his look had touched her. "Sounds wonderful."

Later in her living room, Lisette headed toward her kitchen. "Since you walked me all the way to my apartment, the least I can do is fix you a cup of coffee. It's cold out there."

"Sounds good to me." Colton turned in a full circle, taking in her living room—warm and inviting with a tan couch and two navy blue lounge chairs with an end table between them, all grouped in front of a large fireplace with fake logs stacked on a grate. "May I turn the fireplace on?"

"Sure. After running around in the snow today, it's going to take a lot to totally thaw me out," Lisette said from the kitchen, the scent of coffee drifting through the air.

He stood by the mantel staring at the flames dancing about the pieces of artificial wood. This was one thing he missed when staying in an extended-stay hotel. No fireplaces except down in the lobby. He stepped back, holding his hands out near the fire for a moment before he took a seat on the couch. On one wall there were two bookcases full of books—various fiction titles of different genres as though she couldn't make up her mind which type of story she liked to read the most.

Lisette entered with two mugs, steam wafting from them, and passed one to Colton, then sat in a lounger. She kicked off the flats she'd worn under her snow boots and put her feet up on the footrest. "Ah, this feels good. My feet have been screaming at me to get off them for the past few hours."

"I didn't hear anything," Colton said with a straight face, bringing the cup to his lips and sipping.

"Funny." She chuckled. "Actually, it feels good to laugh."

"After the week we've had, I agree. I like your apartment, especially the fireplace."

"It makes the place feel cozy, which after a day like we just had is what I want." She drank from her mug. "Maxie seemed surprised to see me again. She kept looking at us."

"I know I shouldn't have taken you there a second time, but her food is so good. She's going to have us engaged if I show up a third time with you."

"I'll remember that when you suggest it again."

"We're getting close to finding Saunders. He's getting sloppy. He believes he's thought of everything. Having the woman set up a diversion for his getaway is going to be his downfall. I think it was Hannah Adams, and she hasn't returned home yet this evening. I have a BOLO out on her car, but nothing."

"She might have skipped town. Or they both might have."

"I think Saunders has to stay around here to sell Baby C. Otherwise, he'd have been out of here by now. Before I went in to talk with Jordan this evening, I heard back from Marshal Benson. The fingerprints in the house were

Saunders's. That means he was across and down the street from Buddy Smith, whose prints were there along with a couple of sets that couldn't be matched."

"The first thing I'm going to do when I show up for work at the fertility clinic on Wednesday is get Hannah's fingerprints on an item for you to match the ones in the house. That is, if she shows up for work."

He smiled. "Try to be subtle about it. We don't want you spooking the woman and missing our opportunity to follow her to Saunders."

"What if she doesn't show up?"

"Don't go there. I'm not going to think about that. She'll be there."

"What are you, Susie Sunshine?"

He burst out laughing. "No one has ever accused me of being that."

"Why not? Your attitude about justice and what we do is healthier than mine. I let it get to me. You put it in the Lord's hands."

"You can, too. It's a matter of changing your attitude."

"Ah, I love how easy you make that sound." Lisette cradled the mug between her hands. "I'm still not thawed out."

Colton put his hand on a blanket over the back of the couch. "Here, bundle up in this." He stood and covered the distance between them, then tucked the throw around her. "Better?"

Her gaze linked with his. A softness in her green depths alerted him to the danger of staying. But he couldn't back away. His look fastened onto her lips, and he realized he would kiss her before the night was through. She'd been in the hospital the night before, but instead of resting, she dove right back into the case, staying up with him through everything they had experienced today. The apartment was so quiet he heard a clock ticking from another room, and yet he couldn't move.

"Why do you keep yourself apart from others?"

Her question defused the moment as though he had plunged into a snowbank dressed in shorts and a T-shirt. A shiver rippled down his spine, and he stepped away, until the backs of his legs encountered the couch. He sat, dragging his attention away from those lips.

After a moment, he sliced a look toward her. "I thought we weren't going to pry into each other's life."

"You don't have to tell me. You work well with people, but you don't want to get too close. I was wondering what happened to you to make you like that."

"People disappointing me over and over. In foster care you learn to not expect much. I learned to keep my distance from others. It was easier." Telling her felt right, and that surprised him.

"And lonely."

"I have friends." Even he heard his defensive tone. He knew they weren't really friends but acquaintances. He didn't pry into their lives. Didn't want to. He'd told himself it was because he respected their privacy, but that hadn't been it. When you got to know someone on a deeper level you gave a part of yourself to them.

"Friends you confide in?"

"I confide in God."

"I can't argue with that, but He made us to be social. To be with others."

The more he was around her, the more he realized that was true, and he wasn't very good at it. He had spent a life not being able to protect himself. "I have a question for you. What happened between you and your mother?"

TEN

Lisette shifted in the lounger, snuggled beneath the blanket to ward off the coldness that still infused every part of her. But then she stared at Colton, his question still ringing in her ears, and realized she cared for this man. She hadn't allowed herself to get close to a man since her disastrous relationship with a fellow FBI agent when her world had fallen apart due to her mother's behavior. Chad had been protecting himself, making it clear he hadn't really loved her as he professed because his career was more important that any relationship they'd had.

"That's a fair question. In all my time in the FBI I've never had so much action or so many close calls as I have on this case. It's made me look at my life differently. What I thought was important isn't as much."

"What did you think was important?" Colton relaxed back, mug in hand, as though they were a couple spending a quiet evening together before a warm fire.

But until now there had been nothing quiet about their evening. And she appreciated Colton for being able to do that. From what she'd heard about him, he was used to a lot of intense situations. Except for a few kidnappings, most of her cases had been routine and mundane. "What people thought about me. When my mother left the FBI disgraced and under questionable circumstances, I thought the whole agency was looking at me and waiting for the same thing from me. I'd put myself center stage when in reality I wasn't. You know, one of the first things I thought about when I heard the shot and saw Buddy Smith go down was that I should have talked to my mom, made some attempt to forgive her."

"Have you forgiven her?"

"I'm working on it. We never had a good relationship, especially after my baby sister died. She was a different person after that. Work became everything to her. At the time when I was a child, I felt abandoned even with her nearby. My father left us and I rarely saw him. I spent a lot of time in my hometown with my grandma. New Orleans was my home even though I lived other places most of the year with a mother who wasn't home much."

"Are you going to call her and talk to her?"

"I don't know. I'm afraid she'd hang up on me, but I've got to make the attempt for myself. Maybe when this is over, I'll take some time and go see her."

"I wish my mother was alive. We had a good relationship, but her death ripped that away." His voice quavered. "But I did have one foster mom who really tried to make me a part of her family. I'm the one who fought it. I was seventeen, and after seven years of being rejected or feeling like the means for a foster family to make a little money, I didn't think I belonged anywhere but by myself."

Thinking about their childhood hurts jammed Lisette's throat with emotions that threatened to overwhelm her. She wouldn't cry—hadn't since her mother told her tears only showed her weakness. But they were there in a huge knot demanding release.

Lisette inhaled deep breaths until the constriction about

her chest eased. Then she tossed the blanket off and stood. "But you're never alone with the Lord."

He blinked rapidly as if he hadn't realized that before. "You're right."

She sat on the couch next to him, needing to be near him as though his bodily warmth radiated outward to encompass her. The past forty-eight hours had been rough, but nothing like this. Sharing a part of herself with another seemed far more dangerous. She'd forgotten how to do that since Chad. "I'm glad we talked about our pasts. I think we both needed it. You can't keep it locked up forever. It has a way of coming out when you least expect it."

His mouth quirked into a grin. "You caught me at a rare vulnerable moment. You're good as an interrogator. If you ever need a reference, I'll be glad to give you one."

She nodded. "Well, thank you, sir. I'll have to remember that. Maybe we'll be able to work on another case together."

His smile faded. "I'm interviewing for a position in Dallas or L.A. when this case is over."

"Ah, that's right. You've been here two years. Time to move on." A chill returned, and she started to stand, to end the evening before she lost her heart to someone who didn't want it.

Colton clasped her hand, halting her, and tugged her back down. "Both offices agreed to wait to make a decision until after this was over and I could interview with them."

"Does your Denver office want you to go?"

"No, but…"

"It's become a habit that you move?"

His mouth firmed. "Nothing has been settled. Why are we talking about this?" His hand holding her wrist moved up her arm, and he drew her closer.

The beating of her heart escalated, thudding against her rib cage. She should pull away. She couldn't. His gaze trapped hers and held her tethered to him. He slowly leaned toward her, his other hand coming up and cupping her face. Her throat went dry. She tried to swallow and couldn't.

He hauled her closer. The second his lips pressed against hers, she lost any objectivity concerning Colton Phillips. His mouth claimed hers in a vehement kiss that exemplified the man she'd come to care about. Too much.

She wound her arms around his neck and returned his kiss with welling emotions denied so long she'd forgotten what it felt like to let the walls down even for a few minutes. When he encased her in his embrace, the sensation that she'd come home fluttered through her…and sent off alarms clanging in her mind. He was leaving after this case. She was staying. The walls went up, and she pulled back, her hands clasping his shoulders as if that would keep him away.

He opened his mouth to say something but instead snapped it closed and rose, causing her arms to fall to her sides. "I'd better go. Tomorrow will be another long day, tracking down leads. The longer he has Baby C, the bigger the risk that we won't save her in time."

She started to stand.

He waved her down. "I can let myself out."

She watched him stroll to the door, part of her wanting to call him back. She gritted her teeth to keep the words inside.

Before leaving, he turned toward her, gave her a lopsided grin and said, "I don't regret for one second kissing you." Then he was gone, the click of the door shutting reverberating through the apartment.

I wish I could say that. I think he's taking a piece of my heart with him.

She scrubbed her fingers down her face, trying to erase his mark on her. She couldn't. Tonight had changed everything.

On Wednesday, her first day undercover, the fertility clinic closed for lunch from twelve to one. Lisette glanced at her watch and noted five minutes to go. She realized undercover work would never be something she would jump to do again. Playing someone else was hard for her, but she was doing what she had to as a nurses' aide.

The morning had dragged while she tried to figure out how to get close to Hannah Adams, but the woman kept busy and wasn't one for chitchat. At least she came to work today. She'd been gone Monday and Tuesday. Word around the office was she had been sick.

Lisette hoped Hannah relaxed at noon. She had discovered one thing. Hannah was supposed to meet the receptionist for drinks on Saturday evening and hadn't. That had been the day after the masquerade ball. Had something with Saunders kept her busy?

Shirlee hadn't been pleased with Hannah, and the atmosphere in the office had grown cold. The nurse seemed to be ignoring the narrowed glares directed at her, almost as though she didn't even realize how Shirlee felt about being stood up for a night on the town. At least Lisette had been able to text Colton about Hannah being supposedly sick but looking very healthy today. There had been no word back from him yet. She knew he'd been tied up with following the leads Harrison and Jordan had given them and hours of studying traffic camera footage.

The last patient of the morning left the clinic, and Lisette sighed heavily as she came out of the exam room after sanitizing it.

Hannah laughed. "You'll get use to the mad rush. Wednesday is always busy. Friday will be an easier day."

Lisette smiled. "I felt like I'd jumped into a raging fire this morning, but I'm hoping this will work into a permanent job. I like being busy. Any advice?"

"Don't make plans with a person in the office and not call at least to cancel when you can't make it."

Lisette widened her eyes. "She wasn't too happy with you."

"Yeah, I know. Everyone knows in here. I'm sure even Dr. Martin and Dr. Vincent know. I'm going to have to figure out a way to make it up to Shirlee." Hannah started walking toward the break room.

Lisette fell into step next to her. "It must have been pretty important. Just tell her and apologize. She'll come around."

"You don't know Shirlee. She can hold a grudge." She stopped short of going into the room, glancing inside.

Shirlee sat at a round table with two others.

"Do you want to go to the café on the first floor?" Lisette thought getting her away from the drama in the office would be more conducive to talking.

"You didn't bring anything for lunch?"

"I didn't know about the break room. I figured I had to go out to eat. First days are tough."

"Sure. I'm not relishing eating in the Arctic Circle. Let's go."

Lisette grabbed her purse from the locker assigned to her, noting that Hannah's was two down from hers. Maybe later she would see if she could get into it and find out if there was anything that would help the case. In the meantime, she would pump Hannah for information concerning the clinic. Personal info would have to wait.

Lisette followed Hannah into the café, choosing a salad and can of pop from the choices. This restaurant wasn't anything like Maxie's. It catered to busy medical staff that came in and often took their food and drink with them, but there were some tables and chairs set up for the ones who wanted to eat there. Hannah grabbed the one with a view out the front window onto the parking lot.

"What I like about this café is that the prices are right and the food isn't bad." Hannah took the seat that faced the entrance, leaving Lisette with her back to it.

Lisette avoided facing away from the door in an establishment. The vulnerable sensation of that position whipped down her length, making her go tense.

"Relax. We have plenty of time to eat. This was a good suggestion, Lisa." Hannah used the name Lisette was working under—Lisa Mills.

Lisette scanned the ten-table restaurant and said, "Yes. It's nice getting away from work. Breaks up the day. I saw the list of patients coming in this afternoon. I thought this morning was busy, but it looks worse after lunch."

"Yep." Hannah took a sip of her Coke. "Thursdays are just as bad."

"Tell me about Dr. Vincent. We mostly seem to work for him. Do we ever help with Dr. Martin's patients?"

"Not usually unless there's a shortage and we have the time to help cover. It happens a couple of times a month."

"Dr. Vincent was great with the patients this morning. He takes the time to listen to them."

"He's trying to fulfill their dreams of having a child. He's dedicated to that."

"It sure is needed. I had a good friend who couldn't

have a baby and desperately wanted one. She ended up adopting a little girl from Russia. Another one used the services of a fertility clinic like this one. I was excited to get this opportunity. I know how much it meant to them to be able to have a child."

"Personally I don't see the lure of being a parent, but I'm glad others do. This is a great job working with Dr. Vincent."

"Thanks, Hannah. I've enjoyed this. It beats eating by myself."

"We'll have to do something after work one day this week." Hannah's gaze latched on to something behind Lisette. Hannah stiffened and moved so Lisette blocked her view from someone coming into the restaurant.

"What's wrong?"

"Dr. Freeman just came in. His receptionist usually comes to get his food. He's not too happy with me."

Lisette scooted her chair over to block Hannah better. "It's not fun dodging someone at work. Who's Dr. Freeman? What happened?"

"I wanted to go to a masquerade charity ball and didn't have the money to pay for the ticket. Dr. Freeman's office is in this building and I've seen him around. He's been asking me out for a while now, and I knew he was going so I accepted. But he isn't the guy for me."

Lisette chuckled. "I've been there before. Once I went out on a blind date and had to cut the evening short with an excuse I was sick to my stomach."

"Were you?"

"No, unless you call the roiling in my stomach from listening to his constant bragging being 'sick,' then yeah."

Hannah laughed and when she realized how loud she was, clapped her hand over her mouth and ducked farther behind Lisette. She once did have a blind date who sang his attributes all night long. She'd learned if she ever posed as someone else to keep what she told as close to the truth as possible. And so far she'd been able to.

A minute later, Dr. Freeman stopped at the table, his attention focused on Hannah. "It's nice to see you. Did you ever find your sheep?" A tight thread wove through his words.

"Nope, still lost." Hannah picked up her sandwich and took a big bite.

Grumbling something under his breath, he turned to leave. Lisette dropped her head so he couldn't see her face and stuff a forkful of lettuce into her mouth.

When he disappeared, Hannah giggled. "I told him at the ball I went looking for my sheep I lost instead of spending the night dancing with him. Needless to say, I took a taxi home that night."

"You're bad," Lisette said with a laugh, hoping Dr. Freeman didn't see her enough to recognize her from the ball. He was pretty drunk and probably didn't remember her helping him. "What's this about sheep? What did you dress as?"

"Little Bo Peep. There weren't a lot of costumes left that I could fit into. I'm tiny. So many things have to be hemmed when I go shopping."

"I have the opposite problem. I have long legs. If it fits on top, it often doesn't in the length." As much as Lisette would love to talk about the ball and more things involving why she was here, she didn't want to press too much and raise suspicion, so the rest of the lunch, she and Hannah discussed clothes, then got on the subject of Denver as they were leaving.

At the door Lisette halted. "I forgot to leave a tip."

"You don't have to. It's not like they wait on us."

"Yes, but the food was good and they will have to clean up the table. I used to work as a waitress and know how little they're paid. I'll catch up with you on the stairs."

Hannah shrugged. "Suit yourself. It's your money."

Lisette made sure that Hannah left before she snatched up the soda Hannah drank from and stuck it in a paper bag and then into her big purse. Today was a success—there would be fingerprints on the can. Colton would be able to match it with the ones at the house.

"You two are becoming quite the regular customers. This is the fourth night you've eaten dinner here." Maxie grinned. "Do you need these menus?"

"Actually, I'd like to try something different this evening." Colton took one from Maxie. "What Lisette ordered last night looked delicious so I'm going to have that but—" he paused, giving Lisette the menu "—she's the more adventurous type and wants to get something new tonight, too."

Maxie winked. "My kind of gal. You can't go wrong with anything here, but then I guess I'm partial to this café."

Lisette laughed and without looking at what was offered said, "Surprise me. After the long day I've had, I don't have the energy to try and decide."

When the owner of the café left, Colton covered Lisette's hand on the table. He studied her tired eyes. "You okay?"

"It's hard being someone you're not, and today I couldn't find out anything to help find Baby C. We were so busy, we barely had time to grab lunch, let alone talk. I did get to check Hannah's work area when I went for a chart. I didn't find anything to help us. Did you get a match from the soda can I gave you last night?"

"Yes, Hannah Adams and Harriet Peabody are the same person. We altered a photo of Hannah to match what Harrison told us about the woman who hired him, put it in a photo array and he picked Hannah's photo out. See if tomorrow you can get into her locker. We're checking her phone records and financial ones. If I can find something we can use against her, she might turn on Saunders."

"How about the two doctors who run the clinic? Anything pointing to either one?"

Colton paused for a moment while Maxie brought them decaf coffee, then when she was gone again he said, "Nothing so far and we're digging into their records, too."

"It could be just Hannah. She has expensive taste. I know she gets a good salary with the clinic, but she's living above her means from what I've gathered from the staff and Hannah. Sometimes I feel like I'm back in high school. Those ladies like to gossip."

"Josh McCall is coming tomorrow. They found a tracker in the car I drove to the airport in St. Louis, right where Saunders was sitting. It was stuffed down in the cushion at the back of the seat. They took another look at the three guys involved in the crash. Two were cleared, but the man in the Mustang has disappeared. He thinks it's the same person who turned out the lights in the ballroom. He's bringing what they have on him."

"Can't he email it to us?"

"Yes, but I think Josh is upset they didn't find anything wrong with the man when they checked into him the first time. He had a good cover. He did work at the hospital."

Lisette snapped her fingers. "Another medical connection. If he's here, I wonder if Hannah knows the man. I wish we had a clear photo of him rather than a sketch. Other than the two doctors, we don't have any males working at the clinic. But Shirlee is dating a guy who works in a medical lab in the building."

"Is Hannah dating anyone?"

"She hasn't indicated anyone, but she's receiving calls and texts throughout the day."

"Saunders?"

"Maybe." Lisette smiled at Maxie, inhaling a deep breath. "It smells wonderful. What are you surprising me with?"

"My beef stew."

"Not buffalo stew?" Lisette said with a chuckle.

"No, this is beef. This will put some weight on your bones. You could blow away in a blizzard, child."

Lisette's cheeks flamed. "I've been so busy I forget to eat, but I'm going to enjoy this."

Maxie placed Colton's plate in front of him. "Here's your chicken-fried steak with tons of gravy and mashed potatoes."

When Maxie left, Colton cut a piece of meat, slid it into his mouth and chewed. "Delicious. I'm surprised you didn't order it again tonight."

"Contrary to you, I like variety at least in my food."

"But not where you live? Is that what you're saying?"

"For a guy who likes to eat the same thing over and over, I'm surprised you like to move so often."

His mouth tilted up in a grin. "I can't be too predictable. That would be boring."

"Oh, I don't think you need to worry about that." Lisette scooped up some of the stew. "Let's talk about something other than the case. I've been living and breathing it until it even occupies my dreams."

"Am I in your dreams?" Colton teased, but realized after the question was out that he wanted to know the answer.

She ducked her head. "You're part of the case." When she lifted her chin and ate a bit of her dinner, a rosy tint brushed the tops of her high cheekbones.

The fact he was in her dreams intrigued him. She'd been in a fair share of his dreams in the past week, but he wasn't going to admit that because his never involved the case. One was with Lisette and him finding Baby C. She gave him the child to hold and suddenly he was staring at a baby who looked exactly like he did when he was an infant. When he peered at Lisette, he caught sight of her wedding band, a match to the one on his left hand. He woke up. He'd never dreamed of being married, let alone being a father.

"Colton!"

He blinked. "What?"

She shook her head. "Nothing."

But the tug of her mouth downward shouted the opposite. "Sorry. I was thinking about…"

"What?"

"Nothing. Did you say something?"

"It's not important." She concentrated on what she was eating as though that were the only thing that mattered.

Sitting next to her, Colton touched her arm. "I'm sorry. I got sidetracked."

"A day off. What's that?"

"Something I plan to take when this is over. What were you talking about?" He focused totally on her.

"I called my mother last night."

"You did? What happened? Did you talk long?"

"No. I had to leave a message, but I'm going to try again when this is over with."

"Why not tonight?"

Lisette picked up her coffee and took several sips. "Now that I think about it, there's too much going on for the conversation I want to have with her."

"What if she calls you?" Colton ate some mashed potatoes drenched in cream gravy.

"I don't think she will. We parted on bad terms. I…" Her voice came to a shaky stop. She swallowed hard. "I was so furious with her that I actually think I did something I didn't think I could. I hurt my mother's feelings."

"You can't hurt someone unless they care."

Lisette's eyes grew round. "I remember that look she gave me before getting in the car and driving away. We'd just fought, so we were both angry, but that wasn't what was in her expression. She seemed sad for a moment, then turned away. That's the last time I saw her in six years. She tried calling a few times, and I didn't return her calls." She released the spoon she held, and it clanged into the nearby empty bowl. "I haven't thought about that day in years because it always left me feeling upset…vulnerable. There was a time I thought my mom could do no wrong and I wanted to be just like her. She shattered that, and I couldn't forgive her, but there are times I wondered if there was more to the story than I was told."

"You owe it to yourself to find out." The ashen cast to Lisette's features highlighted her anguish at the memory. Colton wanted to hold her, comfort her, but not in a restaurant full of people. "Let's leave. I'll take you home."

Tears glistening in her eyes, she nodded and prepared to leave while he paid the bill. In the short ride to her apartment, silence hung in the air. It took all his willpower to keep from pulling over and drawing her to him. He felt the hurt as if it were a palpable force swirling around in the car.

After parking, he exited his Jeep and hurried around to open her door. She was halfway out by the time he arrived and lifted her gaze to his. She'd managed to gather her composure while he drove her home, but he knew from experience it was only buried beneath layers of protectiveness. He was an expert at that.

He took her hand and headed for the front of the building.

"We've been through this before. I can walk myself to my apartment." There was none of the teasing tone from the night before.

"I know. It's not for you but me. I'd worry."

"Haven't you said that you're in God's hands? So am I."

"For myself, I don't worry. For others, I do."

She chuckled.

He loved hearing that sound in the crisp winter night. At the elevator he punched her floor, and the doors immediately swished open. "Things must be going our way. No waiting."

A minute later Colton stood in front of her apartment and didn't want to say good-night until he knew she was all right. "I normally don't interfere in other people's business, but I'm going to break one of my rules. Call your mother again. Maybe she was gone last night. Or maybe you'll have to call her several times to get your point across that you want to talk to her."

One corner of her mouth lifted. "I'm stubborn, but my mother is twice as stubborn as I am."

"How important is this to you?"

"I need to do it. The Lord has been right all along. I need to take care of my past, or I'll never be able to be completely happy in my future."

"What if you do get ahold of her and you tell her you

have forgiven her and she refuses to accept it? What if she's still angry with you?"

"Well, then at least I will have done what I needed to do. I can't control her response, only what I do."

He framed her face, looking again into those glittering eyes. "It's okay to cry. I'm not one of those men who can't take a woman crying. It can be good for you."

"Who said I was going to cry?" Her voice quavered.

He touched the corners of her eyes, and one tear rolled down her cheek. "That."

"What have you done to me? I don't cry."

He folded his arms around her and pressed her against his chest. She wept softly. He kissed the top of her head, trying to impart his caring. The sound of her tears cracked the stone wall around his heart, and one by one the blocks crumbled into dust. He stopped short at the thought he was vulnerable again. He'd promised himself he never would be after he realized he'd never find a family like he'd had before his mother died.

She leaned back, staring up into his face. "You *are* bothered. You tensed." She tried to pull away.

He locked his arms about her and said, "No, it's not you."

"Then who?"

"Me. I want you, but I'm not a forever kind of guy. I'd better go." He dropped his arms away and began to turn.

She clutched him. "Wait." Drawing his head around, she stood on tiptoes and whispered her lips across his mouth, then quickly swung around and moved inside.

Colton stood frozen in the hallway, staring at her door. He reached up to knock, curling his hand into a fist, but at the last second changed his mind. This was better. What did he know about a long-term relationship?

* * *

Why in the world had she kissed him? Because she had wanted to all night. She'd exposed her emotions to him, more than she had to anyone. Why him? Why now?

She tossed her purse onto the small table in the entry hall, then made her way to her phone to check her messages before she toyed with Colton's idea of calling her mother again. He was right. She should.

She had five messages on her answering machine—all from the same number, her mother's. She listened to the last one. "Lisette, this is your mom. I'm returning your call. Please call when you come in."

Please. Her mother had rarely said that word, especially those last years before she'd been removed from the FBI. *Has she changed? Or am I reading too much into a word?*

Her hand trembled as she picked up the phone and punched in her mother's phone number. "Mom, I just got in."

"Lisette? You sound different from when I talked to you last."

The tears she'd begun to shed in the hallway returned, blurring her vision. She closed her eyes, hoping to keep them inside. "How are you?"

"Good. I was glad to see you called me yesterday."

You could have called me, she wanted to say, and realized that would lead to a fight, especially since she'd ignored her mom's calls in the past. That wasn't the reason Lisette had phoned her.

"The last time I saw you, we didn't part on good terms," her mom said. "I started to call you many times these past six years, but I just couldn't bring myself to do it. I was wrong. I left you with the impression I had taken some stolen money my partner and I recovered. I didn't."

"Why didn't you tell me that? I asked you."

"I saw your look. You wouldn't have believed me. Besides, I had no proof it was my partner, John, until much later. I took the evidence I found to my former boss and let him know."

"Why didn't you let *me* know?" Her voice rose several levels as she gripped the receiver. Forcing herself to sit in a nearby chair, she drew in fortifying breaths.

"I thought when you were ready to listen you'd call me."

"Then why didn't someone else tell me?"

"I asked my boss to keep it quiet. I didn't want to bring it all up again. Besides, John had a family. They didn't need to be disgraced. He wasn't around to answer for what he'd done, and there would have been some who would have still wondered if I hadn't known what my partner was doing and benefited somehow."

When her mom and partner were working their last case, she hadn't backed up John as she should have—at least, that was what Lisette had been led to believe. "Did you let him be killed?"

"The guy I was bringing in for questioning was working with John. I'd found out he had betrayed me and the FBI, and when I should have responded, I hesitated. John took the bullet for me. I've lived with that for these past years, replaying the shooting in my mind over and over. I suppose that even influenced me to keep quiet about John. Some people would think I was putting the blame on John because I didn't back him up like I should have."

There was a long pause. Lisette couldn't think what to say to her mother.

"Is this why you called yesterday?"

Lisette rubbed her fingers into her forehead. "No. I wanted to tell you that I forgave you for what happened."

It had all been for nothing. With a few words their relationship could have been different.

"Honey, I made a mess of everything. It's my pride. I've been working on it and still have a ways to go. Please don't be mad at me. I tried calling you several times and never could work up the courage. I never thought I was afraid of anything until that first time I hung up before putting in the last number. I didn't want to hear your disappointment in me again. I still feel John wouldn't have died if I had just moved quicker."

Lisette swallowed over and over to coat her parched throat. "There were things I could have done to make the situation better. I jumped to conclusions and then didn't give you a chance to say much. I'm sorry. I forgive you, Mom, but I hope you can forgive me, too. I hope we can see each other soon."

"That's the best news I've heard in a long time. I've been following your career and know the mess I caused hurt your chances in the FBI, but I was able to get my former boss to put your name in for the Denver position."

Her mother had been there in the background all those years—wasted years because of their pride. Lisette finally released the tears she'd been fighting for the past hour.

ELEVEN

Colton greeted Marshal Josh McCall with a handshake. "How was your flight?"

"Bumpy. Storms between here and St. Louis. I've left my return flight open in case you need help. Did you get a chance to read what I sent you on Sam Wilson?"

Sam Wilson was the guy who worked at the hospital in St. Louis and the driver of the Mustang, the car in front of his SUV when the truck hit him. Colton already knew that Saunders had set up that wreck. So was Wilson here to help Saunders in Denver? "Yes. No one knows where Wilson is going for his two-week vacation?" Colton took a seat at the table in the conference room at the U.S. Marshals Office where the file was open to the end of the papers he'd received from Josh. "Is there any connection between the owner of the white Chevy from Missouri and Wilson?"

"The Chevy was a stolen car that wasn't reported until a day ago when its owner returned from being gone for a week. No connection between them that I could find, but then if I was going to steal a car, I would do it from a total stranger."

"But whoever did steal it conveniently did it at a time the man was going to be gone so it wouldn't be reported stolen for a while. Long enough to get out of the state without any problems."

"Yeah, I noticed that. Wilson lived about a mile from the guy. If there's a connection, it could be in a place they frequented. My partner, Serena, is looking further into that. But I think we're safe to say that Wilson stole the car, drove to Denver and is helping Saunders."

"You don't have to stay. We'll find him and Saunders." Colton firmed his mouth, determined that he would rescue Baby C somehow and put Saunders behind bars, this time with no deal with the government.

"I know, but St. Louis let the man go. I feel I need to be here." Josh looked at Colton. "If that's all right with you."

"I'd like your input. My concern is getting Saunders any way we can."

"Where's your FBI partner?"

"She's undercover at a fertility clinic this week as a temporary nurses' aide. We suspect Hannah Adams, a nurse there, is an accomplice of Saunders. She may be his connection to a couple who will buy Baby C."

"I see you've plastered Saunders's photo all over the place as the kidnapper of a baby."

"We had the FBI give that out. We're working behind the scenes. I hope someone sees Saunders and reports his location. Also, if Hannah is helping Saunders, seeing his photo all over the news may cause her to panic and do something foolish. She's already taken Monday and Tuesday off, telling them she was sick, but there's no indication she was. We think she was helping Saunders, especially on Monday, to get away from us."

Josh leaned over and opened his briefcase, then plopped a file on the table. "Here is all the background information I could get on Sam Wilson in a couple of days. We interviewed everyone we could at the hospital and where he lived. He's been in St. Louis for a year, but guess what? He's from Denver."

"Now why am I not surprised by that? Let's exchange files. You can look over what we've come up with so far. Maybe you can find something to help us. Fresh eyes are always welcomed." Colton took the file on Sam Wilson, praying there was a clue to where Saunders was inside. It had been several days since he'd been forced to move Baby C. He felt the trail had gone cold. Fear for the child mushroomed inside him. *What if Saunders has left Denver and Baby C has been sold?*

Friday afternoon Lisette had a break for ten minutes before the next patient came. Everyone else was occupied and concentrating on what she was doing, including Hannah. She might not have a better time to slip into the room where the employees' lockers were and pick the lock on Hannah's. Time was running out for Baby C. She felt like a razor-sharp pendulum was swinging lower and lower toward her. Any second she would be cut—Baby C gone.

No one was in the corridor when she hurried inside. She checked the other side of the row of lockers, then rushed to Hannah's and began working on it. Her heart thumped against her chest at a maddeningly fast pace. Her breathing became shallow, her hands slick with sweat.

When the lock clicked open, she eased the door wide and began rummaging through what was in the locker. First, she went through her purse but little was in the small bag besides her wallet and checkbook. Then she checked a sweater—nothing in the pockets—a brush and some makeup. At the bottom of the metal cabinet, she grasped an address book and flipped through it. The last page had a phone number jotted down with the initials S.W. She grabbed her pen and wrote it on her palm.

A noise in the hallway drifted to her. Someone was coming. She quickly stuffed everything back into the locker and quietly shut it, then started for the door. It opened, and Hannah came into the room.

She smiled at Lisette. "We only have a couple more hours. That's the good news. The bad news is that we have an extra patient to fit into a busy schedule. We'll be staying later this evening in case you have plans."

"Thanks. I'll cancel my plans," Lisette said to cover her next move, taking her cell phone and texting Colton S.W.'s phone number as she walked out of the room.

In the hallway she sent the text, then pocketed her cell phone while her pulse rate began to slow down to a normal pace. Through the next hours of work, she heard back from Colton that they thought it might be Sam Wilson's number and were investigating that possibility.

When the last patient for Dr. Vincent left, Lisette remained in the exam room to clean. She wiped down the leather bed, then drew up a roll of white paper to cover it. Instead of going home, she would be meeting Colton and Josh at the office.

"Oh, good, I caught you before you left, Lisa."

She pivoted toward Hannah in the entrance. "You mentioned going out after work sometime and since you had to cancel prior plans, I'd love for you to go out with me for dinner and drinks. It's Friday. Time to let loose. I could use some unwinding tonight. How about it?"

"Sure. Do you want to give me the address of where you'll be going?"

"Nah. We can go in my car and I'll bring you back to pick up yours afterward. The place is really popular and the parking lot is pretty small. It's a great spot. There's even dancing and live music."

"You have energy to dance?" Lisette said with a laugh.

With her coat on and her purse tucked under her armpit, Hannah stepped to the side to allow Lisette out into the hall. "Well, maybe not, but I like to watch others and the band that plays at Charlie's Roadside Tavern is good."

"Sounds nice. Let me get my stuff." Lisette slid her hand into her jacket pocket and clasped her phone. As she walked back to the locker room, she texted Colton to tell him where she would be and not to wait for her. She'd let him know how it went when she got home.

With a little alcohol in Hannah, she might let something slip.

Colton came back into the conference after spending all afternoon with Josh, searching various pieces of property that Wilson's family owned in the area. Saunders and Baby C were nowhere to be seen. "This isn't a burner phone. They're working on locating Sam Wilson right now. Let's hope he leaves his phone on and is with Saunders when we find him."

Josh sank into a chair. "There isn't much else we can go on from the file so this lead may be it for us."

The secretary entered with a sheet of paper. "This is the location of the cell phone at this moment. They'll keep track of it and let you know if there's a change."

Josh rose. "That was the shortest rest on record. Let's go."

"I'm grabbing Quinn, too, before he leaves." Colton strode to his usual partner's desk in the office.

When Quinn hung up, he got Colton up to speed. "Dead end on the employee we were running down from the lodge. There are no other leads to follow up from the moose logo."

"That's okay. We have Sam Wilson's current location. It's a motel."

"How?"

"A cell number Lisette got from Hannah's locker a while ago."

Quinn stood. "I'm in." As the three walked toward the exit, Quinn continued, "Brad and Mark are waiting for the go-ahead to grab the courier. It looks like she is getting ready to leave Denver."

Colton withdrew his cell and called Mark. "Pick her up. We can't risk her getting away. Bring her in and see what you can get from her. If Saunders or anyone else were going to contact her, they would have by now."

After slipping into the passenger seat of the Jeep, Josh fastened his seat belt. "I've seen how you drive."

"Don't start with me." Colton threw him a mockingly stern look.

"I wonder why she's still hanging around Denver," Quinn asked as he climbed into the backseat.

"Good question to ask her when she's picked up. Maybe she was waiting for the rest of a payment." Colton drove out of the parking lot.

Josh glanced at Colton, then Quinn. "Or waiting for another baby to transport somewhere else."

"We've got to find the middleman and shut down this baby-smuggling ring." The fervent tone in Quinn's voice matched the same passion everyone who was on this case had.

"I still think it's Saunders. He has a lot of people doing his bidding." Colton made a turn at the green stoplight and drove east toward the motel along I-70. When he pulled up to the main doors near the reception desk, he stood. "I'll find out which unit he's in and get a key to open the door."

Colton walked through the automatic sliding glass doors that parted for him and Josh, who accompanied him. Quinn stayed in the car.

Colton approached the woman behind the counter, showing her his badge. "I need information about one of your guests. What room is Sam Wilson in?"

She checked the computer. "There isn't a Sam Wilson here."

Hannah slanted a look at Lisette. "I hope you don't mind. I have to swing by my house first."

"Your house?" Lisette scanned the crossroad they'd gone through a few seconds ago. She was relatively new to Denver, but she didn't believe Hannah was going to her home. In fact, she was driving completely in the opposite direction—east instead of west.

"Yeah, my place is on the way. I've got to change these shoes. My feet are killing me."

"I should have driven, then. You'll be going out of your way to bring me back to the medical center."

"That's okay. I might be able to persuade you to stay out all night. Party with me. I haven't done that in a while."

Lisette liked to have a good time, but not the kind Hannah was implying. She had to remind herself she was playing a role—one that wasn't Lisette Sutton. "If we're gonna stay out all night, I'd better let my roommate know. She tends to worry when I don't show up when expected."

As Hannah came to a stop at a light, Lisette bent forward and dug around in her purse on the floor for her cell phone. When she leaned back, she started to turn it on.

"Toss it out the window," Hannah said in a voice full of steel.

"Excuse me?" Lisette swung her attention to Hannah. She held a gun pointed at Lisette.

"I tracked his phone to this location. Was he staying here?" Colton pocketed his wallet.

The motel clerk looked up from her computer. "Yes, sir. He checked out ten minutes ago."

"Did you see what kind of car he was driving? Do you have its license plate number?"

The woman examined the registration form and showed Colton. "It was a Honda Accord, red. That's the number." She tapped the form.

"Did he say anything about where he was going? Or did you see which way he turned when he left the parking lot?"

"I have to admit I was watching him leave." A blush colored her cheeks. "He was a nice-looking man, and I hated seeing him go. He got into his car and pulled away." She stared off into space. "He went right when he left here." Her mouth twisted and her eyes became slits. "You know, he did the strangest thing."

Starting to turn toward the exit, Colton stopped. "What?"

"He threw his cell phone away in the trash by the door."

Colton exchanged a glance with Josh.

Josh walked to the garbage can and peered inside. "Yep, one is here. Let's put a BOLO out on the car."

After copying down the information about the vehicle, Colton thanked the lady, then strode toward the sliding glass doors, withdrawing his cell phone. When he reached a captain of police in Denver he'd worked with on several cases, he described the Honda Accord and Sam Wilson.

"I need the car found and followed but do not apprehend Sam Wilson. Call me and let me know where he is. Once we're in place, we'll take over." Colton gave the address of the motel. "He left twelve minutes ago and turned right out of the parking lot."

When he hung up, Colton sighed. "I feel like we're looking for a red snowflake in an avalanche."

"Now the waiting begins."

When Colton reached his Jeep, he opened the back door. "Quinn, I want you to process the room Wilson stayed in. If you find anything that might help, let me know. He hasn't been gone long so the room hasn't been cleaned yet."

After Quinn exited the car, Colton climbed behind the steering wheel and started the car. "I'm going right and I'll drive in that direction. Maybe we'll spot Wilson's car."

"Sounds like a plan. I've got to do something. Waiting isn't my favorite part of the job."

"It's possible Wilson is heading to Interstate 70 and going back to St. Louis. His job might be done here."

"Then that's the direction we'll go."

A few minutes later, Colton pulled up behind a long line of cars at a stoplight that was blinking red. As he moved one vehicle at a time toward the intersection, he punched in Lisette's number to see how the evening was going and to let her know about Wilson. After five rings, it went to voice mail. He gestured to his cell phone hooked into the vehicle's dashboard. "Lisette probably can't talk right now, but she's good about texting me back. Let me know what she says."

Once they got through the intersection, the traffic picked up, moving at forty miles an hour. When Colton's cell phone rang, he quickly punched the on button, thinking it was Lisette calling back. He liked keeping in touch with her while she was undercover.

"Colton, Wilson's car was spotted on Interstate 70. He just took Highway 225's exit and is heading south to Aurora," the police captain he knew said.

"Have whoever is following hang back. We're on the interstate and it's not that far to that exit. I need to know if he gets off Highway 225." Colton disconnected with the police captain and accelerated now that he knew where he should go.

When Colton took the exit to Highway 225, the captain called him again. "I'm patching you in with Officer Skinner, who is tailing Wilson. He'll keep you updated."

"Sir, he just got off on Sixth Avenue heading west," the police officer came through the line.

Colton floored his car, determined to catch up with Wilson. In record time he left the highway and veered into the traffic on Sixth Avenue.

"Suspect is turning south on Toledo. Please advise on following. It's a residential area and I might spook him since there aren't as many cars."

Colton glanced at Josh. "This is when I wish patrol cars were unmarked." Looking at the GPS in the vehicle, Colton said to Officer Skinner, "Hang back. See if an officer is near Parkview Drive and Toledo. They could watch to see if Wilson comes out there. If not, that'll mean he is somewhere in the area between Sixth Street and Parkview Drive. I'm a few minutes behind you."

When he turned onto Toledo, Colton saw the officer parked several houses away and pulled up behind him. Leaving his Jeep running but the headlights off, Colton got out and approached the patrol car. It was empty.

* * *

"What in the world are you doing, Hannah?" Lisette asked in a voice full of bewilderment. She had to play dumb as though she didn't know what Hannah was into.

"Duh. Holding you at gunpoint."

"Why? I thought we were becoming friends." Lisette infused a quavering thread through her words while inside she was fighting the panic threatening to take over. It wouldn't get her out of this mess.

"Because you went through my locker."

"What! I'd never do that."

"My stuff was moved in it."

"Then it was one of the other girls."

"You were in the room. You're new. I know the others and trust them."

"Even Shirlee, who's mad at you? She went in there right after lunch. I saw her."

"So did I and I put something in my locker not long after she left. Who are you really?"

"Lisa Mills. I have a driver's license to prove it."

A horn behind Hannah's car honked. She scowled. "Give me your phone and toss your bag into the back."

While Lisette followed her orders, Hannah grabbed her arm and stabbed her with a needle. She tried to strike out at Hannah while the sound of more than one horn blasted the air. Her vision became blurry as a motorist zipped around Hannah's vehicle.

"What…did you…give…" Lisette struggled to stay awake, but a black veil fell over her mind.

Where was Officer Skinner? Colton scanned the area. The house he was parked in front of sat on a curve in the road, and he didn't see any Honda Accord around. The neighboring home had a front hedge that could hide him from peeking around the bend in the road. Colton made his way toward it and spied a uniformed policeman.

"Officer Skinner?" Colton whispered, in case Wilson was nearby.

"Yes." He held a pair of binoculars in the hand he dropped to his side, and faced Colton.

"I'm Marshal Phillips."

"About five minutes ago he parked on the curb in front of a place twelve houses down the street on this side of the street. I hung back so he wouldn't spot my car when he got out." Officer Skinner gestured toward a car sitting under a large bare tree.

"Did he get out?"

"No, he seems to be waiting for someone." He passed Colton the binoculars for him to use.

"On the road, how far back were you from Wilson?" Staring at the red Honda, Colton saw the silhouette of a person behind the steering wheel. The car was turned off and its headlights were off.

"I was at least ten cars back."

"Is someone at the intersection of Toledo and Parkview?"

"Yes, sir."

"Thank you for your help. You'll need to get out of here before someone spots your patrol car. I need all marked cars to pull totally back."

"I'll call the Aurora officer at the Parkview intersection and make sure he does, as well as any other ones in the area."

"I appreciate it."

While the officer pulled his vehicle into the driveway and turned back toward Sixth Avenue, Colton walked to his

Jeep and climbed inside. "We need to coordinate with the local police." He explained to Josh what Officer Skinner told him. "If Wilson is meeting someone, it might be who we're after, and we don't want to scare him. We need unmarked cars in the residential area to keep tabs on what's going down and eyes if Wilson decides to leave. I don't want to lose him."

"I'll set that up while you stand watch."

Colton exited his Jeep again and withdrew his night-vision binoculars. He didn't want to miss anything. "Join me when you have the support in place."

While peering through the binoculars, everything an eerie green, Colton stomped his feet and blew air on his free hand. He'd left his gloves back at the office. When Josh joined him, he murmured, "Will the police be watching all exits out of this neighborhood?"

"Yes, we may need to make the decision to pick Wilson up. He did leave his cell at the hotel, so he must suspect something. This could be a trap."

"Besides Hannah, it's all we have. We may be here for a while. I wish it was a warmer night."

"Or you could have dressed warmer," Josh said with a chuckle.

"I thought my gloves were in the Jeep. Now I remember I left them at the office. I wonder if Wilson heard we were looking into him in St. Louis."

"He shouldn't be surprised that we would check him out since he was there at the wreck in St. Louis."

Josh took the binoculars Colton offered him and examined the scene. Colton studied the rest of the houses on that stretch of Toledo. Was Saunders in one of the houses with Baby C? Who was Wilson waiting for?

He pulled out his cell phone and checked to see if Lisette had left him a text. Nothing. *So why hasn't she?* His last contact with her a couple of hours ago had indicated she would keep him abreast with what was occurring. Maybe he should send a marshal by Charlie's Roadside Tavern on the other side of Denver. As he waited to see what would happen with Wilson, that feeling he should have someone go to the tavern niggled him until he called Janice and asked her to see what was going on with Lisette.

Josh peered through the binoculars. "A car's coming. It's slowing down. Now it's stopping next to Wilson's car. He's getting out—"

Colton took the binoculars to see for himself. "Wilson is going with Hannah Adams. Where's Lisette? She hasn't called and she isn't in the car."

Josh tugged on his arm. "We need to hide. They're coming this way."

Colton, with Josh right behind him, dashed toward the Jeep and ducked inside a few seconds before the headlights indicated Hannah's Taurus was coming around the curve. "When they go by, I'll give them a minute, then we'll follow."

Colton poked his head up and watched Hannah's vehicle disappear around another curve in the road. He started the engine and made a U-turn and began tailing Hannah and Wilson.

"What are they doing together? Going to see Saunders?" Josh asked, then called in the car description and license plate number. When he hung up, he continued, "That's in case we lose them."

"I'm not going to lose him, even if I have to let them know I'm following them. They know where Saunders is. This ends tonight."

When Colton's phone rang, he jerked, taken by surprise by the sudden sound. He'd been so intent on following Hannah's car but keeping himself back far enough they didn't know someone was tailing them. He answered his cell.

"Colton, Lisette isn't at Charlie's Roadside Tavern. I showed a picture and no one has seen her." Worry laced Janice's voice.

"How about Hannah?"

"She hasn't been here tonight, either."

"I want you to track Lisette through her cell phone and let me know what you find." He punched his phone off. "Where is she?"

"Maybe she went home and fell asleep. You two have been pushing yourselves with long hours, not to mention the fact that you were both assaulted just a few days ago. Being undercover takes something from a person. You always have to be on your toes." Josh waved his hand. "Hannah's making a right turn two streets up."

Colton called Janice back. "Have someone or yourself go by Lisette's apartment. Check for her car in the parking lot at the medical center and her place."

When he hung up, he couldn't shake the feeling that something bad had happened to Lisette. Concern embedded deep in Colton's heart and grew. He'd never forgive himself if she were hurt or worse...

The feel of leather against her cheek seeped into Lisette's mind first, then the murmurs of Hannah and a man drifted to her. For a moment, with her eyes still shut, she tried to figure out where she was and what was going on. The motion of the car beneath her riveted her back to what had happened—how long ago?

She didn't want them to know she was awake so she

kept her eyes closed, but slowly awareness of her surroundings and the danger she was in stirred in her. The murmurs became clearer. She focused her attention on what was being said. Maybe then she could figure out what she could do to escape.

"We should just kill her now and get rid of the body." A male voice, deep and gravelly, sent chills down Lisette.

"Saunders will have to decide what to do with her. He thinks she's the FBI agent working with the marshals, which means everything has been blown apart. At least we're leaving town tomorrow after Saunders delivers the baby to the couple," Hannah said from the driver's side of the front seat.

That meant she was still in Hannah's car. When did the man join them? How long had she been out? If Saunders had her fate in his hands, then maybe there was a chance she could convince him to keep her alive. If so, that would buy her some time to come up with a way to escape.

"You had a sweet deal. What are you gonna do? If it hadn't been for her—" the man must have turned to look at her from the way he sounded "—you could have made a lot more money. Your doctor was clueless as to what was going on."

"We'll start over in another town. There are couples everywhere who want babies and are willing to pay."

"What about the people in St. Louis?"

"Saunders says as long as he keeps quiet and stays out of their territory, they'll leave him alone. If nothing else, there's room overseas. Selling this baby will give us the rest of the money we need to start fresh."

"You two worked well together. You supplied the couples and he the babies from his network. How do you know he can do that again?"

"What difference is it to you?" A defensive tone entered Hannah's voice.

"Because I've been asked to kill Saunders."

Lisette's breath jammed her throat. She tested her bound hands tied in front, twisting them, but the rope bit into her flesh. This wasn't going to end well.

TWELVE

His headlights off, Colton inched up to the edge of a warehouse to see where Hannah was going. She parked next to a door into a building beside the one they were at. In the glow from the streetlamp, it appeared abandoned with windows broken out and debris littering the vacant parking lot in front.

"I guess Saunders likes warehouses. That's where he held Annie Duncan and her daughter captive in St. Louis," Josh said while Colton backed up a few feet.

"The house didn't work out for him so he must have decided to go back to what he's used to. That is, if Saunders is inside. If not, we'll arrest these two and give them a deal they can't refuse for Saunders's location. The warehouse, especially one not being used, will be easier to breach without anyone knowing."

Out of view of Hannah's car, the interior light wouldn't give him away when Colton exited his Jeep, grabbing his cell phone and putting it on Silent. He hadn't heard from Janice and needed to know that Lisette was safe at her apartment.

He crept to the corner of the building and peered toward where the car was parked. Wilson climbed from the front passenger's side at the same time Hannah did from the driver's side. He rounded the rear of the vehicle while she opened the back door and pulled on something.

Colton's cell vibrated in his pocket. He kept his gaze trained on what was going on with Hannah and Wilson, but he answered the call. "Phillips here."

"I found Lisette's cell tossed by the side of the road, and she isn't at her apartment."

As Janice spoke, Colton witnessed Wilson helping Hannah drag a bound person from the backseat of the Taurus. "I think she's with the two we're following. They're at a warehouse and taking a limp body into it on the west side." He gave Janice the address. "I need backup. No sirens. Josh and I are going to try to get in and check it out. I want a net put around this place so if Saunders, Hannah or Wilson leave the warehouse, they're caught."

"Don't worry. It'll be done."

Wilson hefted the person into his arms, her head hanging over his arm, a long ponytail tumbling down. Colton tensed, his hands going clammy. *Lisette.* She'd been wearing her hair that way lately. He thrust his phone into his pocket and withdrew his gun from its holster.

"That's Lisette. Once they're inside, we'll find a way in." Colton walked back to his Jeep and got his night-vision goggles in case he needed them in the dark building. From this angle, he didn't see any lights on. If Saunders was in the warehouse—and Colton prayed he was—Saunders would have some kind of illumination but it might be in an inside room.

He returned to Josh, who glanced back. "Have they gone in?"

"Yes."

"Let's go around back where no one can see us from the street." As Colton ran toward the alley between buildings, he prayed the limp body Wilson held was an unconscious Lisette. He shoved any thoughts she might be dead from his mind, or he might not be able to do what was necessary.

The echo of footsteps reverberated through the darkness as Hannah and the man carrying Lisette hurried forward. Lisette remained as limp as possible, although the guy jostled her as he moved. Not a word was spoken, which tempted her to open her eyes and see where they were going. While they had climbed out of the front seat, she'd risked a peek and seen a wooden building with a door near Hannah's car. She wasn't being taken to a house.

Even though her eyes were closed, she knew when she was brought into a brightly lit area of the place.

Then Hannah spoke. "You got her to sleep."

"Yeah, finally. I've never seen a baby cry so much."

Saunders's voice. Should she be afraid or relieved? He didn't try to kill her at the cabin, so she prayed he wouldn't here.

"Good to see you again, Wilson."

Lisette heard the sound of patting as if Saunders and Wilson had embraced.

"I appreciate knowing about the contract out on me. After all I've done for them, it would have been nice if they had trusted me not to turn them in."

Who? Lisette screamed the question in her mind.

A buzzer sounded.

"What's that?" Wilson asked, and plopped Lisette down onto a couch—at least, she thought it was by the feel of the cushions beneath her.

"We've got company. I rigged the doors to alert me when someone was coming inside the warehouse. Let's give whoever is trespassing a warm welcome. Hannah, stay here and take care of the baby and our guarantee we'll get away without a problem."

So that's what I am to Saunders.

Then Lisette realized if someone was coming to her rescue, Saunders had nothing to lose in taking them out. He was looking at life in prison with all the crimes he'd committed, and if he could kill one of his own team members, then others wouldn't be spared, especially when her usefulness was over.

Colton picked the lock on the warehouse and eased the door open. Pitch-blackness greeted him. Colton slipped on his night-vision goggles, wishing he had a second pair for Josh, and inspected the entrance before he entered. He spied a new-looking wire, strung up above and across the ceiling.

He leaned toward Josh and whispered into his ear, "They know we're here. Stay close. We need to move fast before someone comes to check."

When Josh came inside, Colton shut the door quietly. Gun drawn and ready to use, he made his way to the left with Josh following. A faint sound caught his attention ten yards away, and he ducked into a room near the back entrance to the warehouse.

Out of the dark shadows crept Saunders, armed, with Wilson beside him, his weapon in his hand. Saunders had on night-vision goggles and, like Colton, led the way. Saunders made a sweeping inspection of the area in front of the exit. Then he swiveled his attention toward where he and Josh hid, the first room near the back door. Colton dropped back into the room and flattened himself against the wall. He listened.

Again the faint sound of footfalls came closer. He froze, preparing for Saunders to investigate every place a person could hide.

* * *

Saunders had been gone maybe a minute. Lisette wanted to open her eyes to see where Hannah was in the room, but she couldn't, no matter how strong the urge was. But she listened for any noise that indicated where the young woman was—and for gunshots.

Please, God, keep Colton safe. Or whoever has come into the warehouse.

The baby started whining. Hannah swore and, from the sound of her footsteps, crossed to wherever Baby C was.

"Shh. You're all right," Hannah said in a soft singsong voice.

This was her chance, while Hannah was preoccupied with the child. They might have bound her hands but not her legs. She inched her eyelids up and scanned the area around her. The room must have at one time been an office. A desk still sat off to the side.

Where are Hannah and Baby C?

Lisette lifted her head to look over the end of the dirty, musty-smelling couch. In the far corner stood Hannah in front of a carrier, holding Baby C and patting her on the back. Hannah was turned away, her gun stuck in the back of her pants. Lisette scanned for another weapon. Nothing.

Okay, it's now or never.

Her gazed zeroed in on the closed door. One. Two. Three. She launched herself from the couch, ignoring the light-headedness from whatever drug she'd been given, and charged across the room. Grasping the knob with her tied hands, she managed to turn it. With a glance over her shoulder, Lisette plunged into the darkness as Hannah pulled the trigger, the sound of the shot exploding in the air.

* * *

A shot blasted from somewhere in the cavernous warehouse. *No! Please, Lord, not Lisette or the baby.*

The thought it could be one of them hurt or dead ignited both anger and pain inside Colton. He squashed what emotions he could in order to function, but he couldn't quite succeed as he had in the past. Penned down, he was trapped while Lisette might be in trouble. Colton heard the movement outside the room. His breath bottled in his lungs, he readied his body to spring at the first person coming through the door. Josh would take care of the second one.

An arm holding a gun came into view first, quickly followed by the rest of Saunders. Colton leaped toward the man, knocking Saunders's weapon from his hand and tackling him to the floor. The revolver skidded across the room.

Saunders latched on to Colton's arm that held his Wilson Combat, trying to grasp it. Colton rolled with Saunders, wrestling for control of his gun. To Colton's side, noises of bodies clashing filled the air, but he concentrated on his opponent, intent on disarming him. Thoughts of Lisette and Baby C spurred an extra burst of adrenaline to rush through him.

Colton ended up on top of Saunders, his gun wavering between them. He poured his strength into his hand, his fingers digging into the man's flesh like a claw. Saunders groaned and tried to break the viselike grip Colton had on him. He pressed his body into Saunders, squeezing the air from his lungs. Slowly the kidnapper's grasp weakened. Colton went in to finish him off. Jerking his arm with the gun away, he balled his hand and smashed his fist into Saunders's jaw. Once. Twice. The man sagged. Colton hit him again, then quickly rotated him over and clapped handcuffs on him. After removing his night-vision goggles, he clicked on his flashlight, checking to see if Josh needed help. He didn't. He finished securing Wilson while Colton found the light switch and flipped it on.

Now to find Lisette and Baby C.

Fury consuming him, Colton grabbed Saunders and hauled him to his feet. "Show me where Lisette and the child are. And for your sake they better be unharmed."

Saunders threw him a glare. "Sure."

"And I know about Hannah. I hope she cares about you." Colton pressed the muzzle of his gun against the man's temple enough that it left a mark on his forehead.

"You wouldn't." He gave a shaky cackle.

"Don't test me. If anything has happened to Lisette or the baby, I…" He couldn't vocalize the feelings rampaging through him.

Josh dragged Wilson to his feet and trailed Colton from the room. The sound of a baby crying reverberated through the warehouse.

"You better hope Hannah didn't do anything foolish." Colton almost growled the words in Saunders's ears.

The sound of the child's wails ricocheted off the walls, surrounding them in the noise.

"See, she's alive. She's always crying. That's why I'm holed up in an abandoned warehouse."

Which meant that Lisette may not be. Colton's heart ripped in two pieces at that thought.

"We don't know she's dead," Josh said behind him.

The words reminded Colton he had a job to do, a child to save—and, he hoped, an FBI agent.

Following the bawling, Colton didn't even need Saunders to show him the way. When they reached an interior office, the door was wide-open and light streamed out into

the blackness. The frown on Saunders's face deepened.
The expression heightened Colton's concern.

He gave Saunders to Josh, then he flattened himself
against the wall of the office, took two fortifying breaths
and swung into the entrance. The room was empty except
the baby in a drawer on the floor in the corner, her arms
flailing, her face red.

No Hannah.

No Lisette.

The bullet had torn through Lisette's arm, intense pain
piercing her as if a branding iron had seared her. But she
kept going into the black void, zigzagging to throw Hannah
off. Blood flowed from the wound, running down her arm.

Her wounded arm bumped into a pole. She swallowed
a cry, but the throbbing intensity threatened to engulf her.
With her good hand, she used it to feel her surroundings.
She couldn't afford to knock herself out. She increased
her pace as much as she could, hoping she wasn't going
deeper into the warehouse.

Her fingertips encountered a rough wooden surface.
A wall? To a room or the outside? She charged down its
length, praying for a door. Suddenly something in her path
threw her off balance, and she tumbled to the concrete
floor. Her injured arm cushioned her fall.

She sucked in a scream, but a gasp escaped.

Then through the thundering of her heartbeat in her
head she heard them. Footsteps coming toward her.

While Josh guarded Saunders and Wilson, Colton
donned his night-vision goggles and headed into the dark
depths of the warehouse in the opposite direction they

had arrived at the office. He had quickly spotted a trail of blood and began following it.

He tried not to think of Lisette being wounded, but he couldn't stop himself. Emotions he didn't want to feel swamped him. He cared for her. No, it was worse than that. Did he love her? Whenever he had cared and loved someone in the past, they died or left him. He didn't want to go through that again.

He tried to harden his heart as he searched the dark shadows. But all he found was hurt.

The drops of blood increased. Someone was bleeding more and more. His heart thudded against his rib cage, making breathing difficult.

Please, Lord, don't let me be too late.

Frantically Lisette felt what she had fallen over—a tarp covering some crates. She raised the edge of it and buried herself beneath it, putting some of the wooden boxes between her and whoever was coming after her.

The click of Hannah's shoes—she remembered hearing them in the hallway at the fertility clinic—came closer.

Then stopped.

Holding her breath, she prayed to God, putting her life in His hands.

"I know you're in there. Come out and I won't shoot randomly into the tarp."

Hannah's words froze Lisette. Part of her knew the wisdom in what she said, but the other wanted to continue to hold out. She was more valuable to them alive than dead— at least until they left Denver. And she hoped that whoever had come into the warehouse could rescue her in time.

A gunshot went off, close by, striking the tarp and crate

where she'd been a few minutes before. Her teeth dug into her lower lip.

"That one didn't hit you but the next or the one after will."

Lisette put her hand on the cold floor to push herself up.

"Drop your gun or I'll shoot," came Colton's voice.

The most beautiful sound Lisette had heard. She sagged onto the freezing concrete, all energy draining from her body. Her eyelids fluttered closed.

"Lisette. Lisette, don't you dare die on me."

Colton's words penetrated her pain-laced mind. She wanted to surrender to the blackness, but she couldn't. She eased her eyes open and light flooded her vision. She blinked rapidly and closed them again.

"Shut some of those lights off," Colton shouted. "Okay, it's darker now."

"Where's Hannah?" she asked when she looked into his dear face. If one of her arms hadn't been throbbing as though on fire, she'd throw both of them around him and hug him for as long as he allowed it.

He gave her a lopsided grin, but she saw the worry in his eyes. "She's being taken in right now along with Saunders and Wilson. The paramedics just arrived on the scene. They'll get you to the hospital, and you'll be good as new in no time."

"Who are you trying to convince?" Lisette licked her dry lips, wanting to stay conscious and hear all the details, but the edges of darkness again crept closer and finally swallowed her.

A week later Lisette paced her living room, her left arm in a sling from the gunshot wound, dressed for her interview with a television reporter in—she checked her watch—an hour. Having been in the hospital, then at home most of the past week, she was itching to get back to work, even if it was desk duty until her arm healed totally. She was right-handed so it hadn't affected her ability to use a gun.

She was waiting for Colton to brief her on the case before she talked with the reporter. She was to do the interview because of his ongoing work with the Witness Protection Program. She'd seen Colton when she'd come out of surgery on her arm and then several times since then, but always when people were around. They hadn't been alone to talk since the night at the warehouse.

But if nothing else, she realized she loved him. She needed to see him. He'd saved her life, and she hadn't even been able to thank him.

There was a part of her that wondered if he was avoiding being alone with her. The night in the warehouse had been intense, but in the end successful. Baby C was safe. The reason Lisette had agreed to do this interview was to get word out about her. Her parents had to be out there somewhere. She refused to think they had sold the child.

When a rap sounded at her door, she hurried and answered it. Again, she couldn't throw both of her arms around Colton, but she did with the one that wasn't in a sling.

"It's good to see you," she murmured, his warmth pressed against her being exactly what she needed.

He pulled away before she wanted him to. "It's good to see you out of the hospital and on the road to recovery."

"Frankly, I'm getting tired of looking at these four walls."

"Whereas I haven't been at my place much this past week."

"Tying up this case?"

"Yes. We don't know who is behind the ring, but we did find out Saunders was the middleman he called Jackson. We'll be working on him to get him to turn on his bosses. He refuses, but maybe some time behind bars will convince him."

"What about Wilson and Hannah? Do they know the people behind this baby-smuggling network?" Lisette moved to her couch and sat at one end, hoping Colton would join her on the sofa.

He didn't. He sat in a chair across from her. "No. Each one said Saunders does but that he never told them."

"You believe them?"

He shrugged. "They answered questions while hooked up to a lie detector."

"Did Saunders kill Buddy Smith?"

"According to Hannah, although she didn't see him. We're building a case based on motive, opportunity and evidence. We won't need her testimony, and we have plenty on her to put her away for a long time. She and Saunders are responsible for Benjamin Mason's death. Although he didn't die from the head wound, he had a heart attack in the middle of the diversion Saunders had created to occupy us while they got away. That's another death he is responsible for and will be tried for."

Across the short space between them an invisible barrier was being erected by Colton. He'd look at her for a few seconds, then his gaze would slide away as though the sight of her made him uncomfortable. She needed to break down that wall.

"What has the courier told you about Baby C?"

"Not a lot. She picked the baby up at a Houston motel with little security. The person who rented the room for the night paid cash. The clerk couldn't tell the Houston police much about the man. The courier described her contact as wearing sunglasses, a few inches taller than her, which makes the man five ten, and he had dark short hair. They are pursuing the lead but don't have a lot to go on."

At least they had a city to start looking for the child's parents. "Was Hannah acting alone at the clinic? She said so in the car with Wilson but I've learned not to trust everything people say."

"Yes. We've delved into the finances of the people at her work, and there isn't any indication she had help, but your agency will be keeping an eye on the fertility clinic just to make sure. Hannah insisted no one else was involved. She found the clients for Saunders, and he supplied the babies."

She shivered at the thought of what that man had done. "At least he'll get what he deserves, but a lot of people suffered at his hands in a short period of time. Thankfully Baby C is safe. That's what is important."

Colton slapped his hands on the tops of his thighs and pushed up. "And I have to be going. I have a plane to catch."

Her heart cracked. "Dallas?"

"Yes. My interview is early tomorrow morning."

"Why are you leaving Denver? You're responsible for bringing down an arm of the smuggling network. Baby C hopefully will be reunited with her parents soon." Lisette swallowed several times and added, "I'm falling in love with you, and I think you care about me. Stick around and let's see where it takes us. It's okay to stay more than two years in a city." She'd debated all day whether to tell him how she felt, but she would regret it if she didn't.

"The Dallas office has waited to interview me until the case was finished. I owe it to them to go."

And leave me. Hurt at his words swelled her throat, making it difficult to say anything.

"I won't deny I have feelings for you, but maybe it's for the best if I move to Dallas. If we're meant to be, we'll get together long-distance." Pain laced his voice. He looked away, swallowing hard over and over.

"You believe that," came out in a bare whisper. Rising, she averted her head so he wouldn't see the tears gathering in her eyes.

"I don't know what to believe. I almost lost you at the warehouse. I can't lose…"

She slanted a look at him. "So you would rather be alone rather than be with someone because you might lose them sometime in the future? Loss is part of life, but so is love."

He frowned and strode toward the front door. "I'm going to be late for my flight."

Before he left, she clasped his arm and stopped him. "Are you going to be back tomorrow night?"

"Yes."

"Then let's have dinner together at Maxie's at seven. At least one last time. I don't want to say goodbye like this."

He didn't reply. The doorbell rang, and he opened it to find a reporter with her cameraman standing in the hallway. "I'll talk to you later. I'm glad you're better."

She tried to smile, but it lasted a second and then fell. "Safe trip."

When he walked away, she opened the door wider and invited the reporter and cameraman into her apartment.

"Thank you for agreeing to do this interview," the reporter said, directing her cameraman to set up for the taped interview that would air later that night on the local news.

"Excuse me for a moment." Lisette didn't wait for them to say anything but escaped into her bedroom.

She sat on her bed for a moment, composing herself. Her emotions felt as if they were on the edge of a cliff, any wrong word sending them over the ledge into the abyss. She would be at Maxie's tomorrow night, but from the closed look Colton gave her when he left, she didn't think he would be.

When she reentered her living room, she watched as the cameraman and the reporter set up the lighting and a place where the interview would occur. If she wasn't so anxious to do her part to reunite Baby C with her parents, she would have declined the request. But this was important to her.

Seated across from the reporter, Lisette answered her questions about how Baby C came into the custody of the state.

"Any last words for the audience?"

Lisette looked directly at the camera. "I'm asking the public to help the FBI find Baby C's parents." She held up a photo of the child. "She is about three or four months old. Adorable. And she needs her family. The flight taken by the woman who bought Baby C. to Denver originated in Houston, where she boarded with the child. If you have any information, please contact the number at the end of this interview. Help us to reunite the child with her parents and put a stop to baby-smuggling rings." Lisette didn't go into detail that the courier couldn't tell the authorities much about Baby C.

Somehow Lisette made it through the interview and saying goodbye to the reporter and cameraman without shedding any tears, but now that she was alone they ran down her face and she let them. She needed to cry with all that had happened in the past few weeks. They had caught part of the baby-smuggling ring and had done some good work. This would look good on her record, and she didn't care. Her career wasn't who she was. She used to think it defined her. Not anymore. She needed more to make her happy.

A vision of Colton on a plane for Dallas filled her mind. He'd opened her to love again. She would always be indebted to him for that, but why couldn't he see they belonged together? She'd shared things with him she never had with another. Because of him, she and her mother might have a relationship again.

When the phone rang, she considered not answering, but it might be her boss wanting to know how the interview went. When she saw the caller ID, she snatched up the receiver. "Hello."

"This is Marshal Benson. Colton is getting on the plane and can't call you, but I wanted to tell you before you heard elsewhere that Saunders escaped the transport taking him to prison."

For a moment the sound of the words registered on her mind but not the meaning. "He's gone?"

"Yes, we're helping the police with the manhunt. The fact that someone knew he was being transported at that time and route, though, leads us to believe he had someone with clout helping him."

"The people who run the smuggling ring?" Her first thought was she might be in danger, but she really didn't think so. Saunders had no reason to come after her and every reason to escape the area, possibly the country. But in case she was wrong, she would keep her gun on her.

"Most likely. No telling where he is by now."

When she hung up, all she wanted to do was talk with Colton. But she couldn't.

Maxie greeted Lisette at the door into the café. "It's nice to see you. Will Colton be joining you this evening for dinner?"

"I don't know. He's been in Dallas today."

"I have a cozy table for two over here for privacy, if he comes."

If he comes. Those words echoed through Lisette's head as she took a seat, facing away from the door. Otherwise, she would sit and watch people come in and be disappointed every time that it wasn't Colton.

"I'll order in fifteen minutes. Just bring me a cup of your decaf coffee for now, please."

Lisette thought about the day at work with updates on the search for Saunders. He had disappeared. There had been no sighting of him, although his photo had been plastered everywhere in the media. There were also no leads to Baby C's family, but many people had come forward wanting to adopt the child. At least she would have parents one way or another.

"Are you ready to order?" Maxie asked.

Lisette glanced over her shoulder at the door. No Colton. She had to accept this was his answer to her. He didn't want to risk his heart. "Yes, I'll have a buffalo burger with onion rings."

When Maxie left, Lisette dropped her head and kneaded the tight cores of her neck and shoulders. She searched her mind for something to think about that had nothing to do with Colton or her job. For a long time, she came up empty, only emphasizing how much she had allowed her work to take over her life.

A hand clasped her shoulder. Lisette gasped and swung around to find Colton standing behind her with a smile on his tired face. "You're here," was all she could think to say to him.

He brought the chair across from her around the table to sit beside her. "I'm sorry I was late. The plane was delayed and landed an hour late, then there was a wreck on I-70. I tried calling you. I did leave a message on your cell."

"You did?" She rummaged in her purse and found her phone. "I forgot to turn the ringer on after my meeting with my boss at work." She noted a message from him was waiting on her cell.

Taking her hand, he asked, "Have you ordered yet?"

She nodded, a part of her still stunned that he was here. "How was Dallas?" she finally asked, all of a sudden not wanting to broach the subject of their relationship. But he was here. *That's a good sign, isn't it?*

Maxie brought Lisette her food. "I was getting worried about you. What would you like to order?"

"I'll have the special." His gaze captured Lisette's.

A warmth spread through her body. The look in his eyes melted her. But she waited until Maxie left before asking, "Are you moving to the Dallas office?"

"Nope. Not what I want."

"Ah, so you'll wait to see how L.A. is?"

"Nope. Not what I want."

She gulped, her mouth dry. "What do you want?"

"You. I had some time yesterday and today to think about what you said. About these past weeks. I realized I've been a coward. I've been scared to risk getting involved with someone because that meant I would expose myself to being hurt again. My childhood was full of that and I didn't want to go through adult life the same way. I didn't set out to fall in love with you, but I did. My running away to Dallas or L.A. won't change that. I love you, Lisette. I want to marry you. Will you take a chance on me?"

"No."

His jaw dropped.

She hurriedly added, "I mean that I know I'm not taking a chance when it comes to you. I know you. I trust you. I love you and want to share the rest of my life with you. I've never shared myself with another like you. It must be those long hours working together."

"I knew surveillance was a useful tool for a law enforcement officer."

She laughed and placed her other hand on top of his. "You understand me."

He brushed her hair behind her ear, his fingertips grazing down her cheek. Then he tugged her closer. His mouth settled over hers. She poured all her bottled-up longings into that kiss, the pieces of her shattered heart mending together.

* * * * *

Dear Reader,

This is the second book in the new continuity series about U.S. Marshals and a baby-smuggling ring. I can't think of anything worse than losing a baby and trying to find your child. I loved working with the other authors on this series. A huge thank-you to Shirlee McCoy, Liz Johnson, Sharon Dunn, Valerie Hansen and Terri Reed. You are great to work with.

I love hearing from readers. You can contact me at margaretdaley@gmail.com or at 1316 S. Peoria Ave., Tulsa, OK 74120. You can also learn more about my books at www.margaretdaley.com. I have an online quarterly newsletter that you can sign up for on my website.

Best wishes,

Margaret Daley

Questions for Discussion

1. Colton Phillips has been a loner most of his life. He was a foster kid early in life and used to being shuffled from one home to another. He didn't know how to put down roots in one place. In fact, he purposely moved every two years, if not sooner. Are you used to staying in one place or moving around like Colton? Is this what you want? If not, how are you dealing with the situation?

2. What is your favorite scene? Why?

3. Lisette Sutton has learned not to trust others, starting with her relationship with her mother and later with a boyfriend who betrayed her. She's been hurt and holds herself back from others. Has this happened to you? How did you get over the distrust in others? If you didn't, how is it affecting you?

4. Colton refuses to get emotionally close to the people he works with. He knows he will move on soon and it makes it easier when he hasn't invested himself emotionally in his life. Do you do that? If so, how is that affecting you? If not, why do you put yourself out there emotionally with your fellow workers?

5. Who is your favorite character? Why?

6. This series is about selling babies. Some of the children were sold. Others were kidnapped. For a parent

whose baby has been missing, how would you help that person cope with the situation?

7. Lisette felt she had to prove herself constantly in the FBI because of her mother. Have you ever felt that way—that you had to prove yourself because of who you are? How did you deal with this?

8. Lisette needed to forgive her mother in order to move on in her life. This was difficult because she had a hard time letting the past go. Have you dealt with something like this with another person? How did you resolve it? If you did, how has it affected you?

9. Both Colton and Lisette dealt with some hard issues from their past. Lisette questioned her faith while Colton's belief in the Lord strengthened him. How has your faith been tested? How did you resolve it?

10. Lisette was hurt at the end and this scared Colton. He realized he was in love with her, and was afraid of that feeling. He didn't get emotionally close to others because he was hurt as a child. How can he get past that? What kind of life would he have if he never got close to others?

11. Trust is important in a relationship. Neither Colton nor Lisette trusted easily with the job they had and the issues from their past. Has anyone caused you to distrust him or her? Why? How did you settle it?

12. Lisette went undercover at a fertility clinic. She wasn't comfortable playing a role, but she did it because this

was important to finding out information about the missing baby. Have you ever had to do something at your job that you struggled with but knew it was important you did it well? What helped you do it?

13. Lisette is a by-the-book FBI agent while Colton is much more flexible. Which are you—needing to be in control with boundaries or someone who can change if needed quickly, someone who can go with the flow? How has it worked for you?

14. Colton and Lisette had to deal with a criminal who might get a break if he offered testimony and help in taking down someone bigger in the organization. This man kidnapped a child to help him get away and give him money. How would you deal with that situation, trying to protect a criminal who had done some bad things?

15. Do you agree with the government making deals with lesser criminals to catch bigger ones? Why or why not?

REQUEST YOUR FREE BOOKS!
2 FREE RIVETING INSPIRATIONAL NOVELS
PLUS 2 FREE MYSTERY GIFTS

YES! Please send me 2 FREE Love Inspired® Suspense novels and my 2 FREE mystery gifts (gifts are worth about $10). After receiving them, if I don't wish to receive any more books, I can return the shipping statement marked "cancel." If I don't cancel, I will receive 4 brand-new novels every month and be billed just $4.74 per book in the U.S. or $5.24 per book in Canada. That's a savings of at least 21% off the cover price. It's quite a bargain! Shipping and handling is just 50¢ per book in the U.S. and 75¢ per book in Canada.* I understand that accepting the 2 free books and gifts places me under no obligation to buy anything. I can always return a shipment and cancel at any time. Even if I never buy another book, the two free books and gifts are mine to keep forever.

123/323 IDN F5AC

Name	(PLEASE PRINT)

	Apt. #
Address	

City	State/Prov.	Zip/Postal Code

Signature (if under 18, a parent or guardian must sign)

Mail to the **Harlequin® Reader Service:**
IN U.S.A.: P.O. Box 1867, Buffalo, NY 14240-1867
IN CANADA: P.O. Box 609, Fort Erie, Ontario L2A 5X3

**Are you a current subscriber to Love Inspired Suspense books
and want to receive the larger-print edition?
Call 1-800-873-8635 or visit www.ReaderService.com.**

* Terms and prices subject to change without notice. Prices do not include applicable taxes. Sales tax applicable in N.Y. Canadian residents will be charged applicable taxes. Offer not valid in Quebec. This offer is limited to one order per household. Not valid for current subscribers to Love Inspired Suspense books. All orders subject to credit approval. Credit or debit balances in a customer's account(s) may be offset by any other outstanding balance owed by or to the customer. Please allow 4 to 6 weeks for delivery. Offer available while quantities last.

Your Privacy—The Harlequin® Reader Service is committed to protecting your privacy. Our Privacy Policy is available online at www.ReaderService.com or upon request from the Harlequin Reader Service.
We make a portion of our mailing list available to reputable third parties that offer products we believe may interest you. If you prefer that we not exchange your name with third parties, or if you wish to clarify or modify your communication preferences, please visit us at www.ReaderService.com/consumerschoice or write to us at Harlequin Reader Service Preference Service, P.O. Box 9062, Buffalo, NY 14269. Include your complete name and address.

LIS13R

Everything before that moment was blank.

It took considerable effort, but she pried her right eye open far enough to cringe at the glaring light wedged between white ceiling tiles. Pain sliced like a knife at her temple. She tried to lift her hand to press it to her skull. Maybe that would keep it from shattering. But her arm had tripled in size and weighed more than a beached whale. She could only lift it an inch from where it lay at her side.

Fire shot from her elbow to the tip of her middle finger, a sob escaping from somewhere deep in her chest and leaving a scar inside her throat as it escaped.

"Julie?"

Julie? She turned to look in the direction of the voice to see who else was in the room, but something plastic tugged against her nose. An oxygen mask. She didn't even try to lift her hand to adjust it, instead rolling her eyes as far as she could.

A gentle hand with cold fingers pressed against her forearm, but the face was just out of reach. "Julie? How are you feeling?"

Who was Julie? There wasn't anyone else in her limited line of sight, but that didn't mean the other girl wasn't close by.

A face—round and blurry—appeared right above her. Wide-set blue eyes shone with compassion and the same brilliance as her white smile. "I'm Tammy, your ICU nurse." Cool fingers secured the cannula back into place and brushed across her forehead.

What was she doing in the ICU? On a hospital bed in the ICU? And why had the nurse been calling her Julie?

That wasn't her name.

"I know someone who's been looking forward to talking with you. If you're ready, I'm going to let Detective Jones know that he can come in and see you. He's been waiting to talk with you for three days."

She tried to shake her head. A detective? As in a police officer? Why were the police coming to see her? What had she done?

Can Julie remember her past to save her future?
Pick up STOLEN MEMORIES wherever
Love Inspired Suspense books are sold to find out.

LISEXP0214

RB ✗ JLB
CB

Love Inspired

SUSPENSE
RIVETING INSPIRATIONAL ROMANCE

THREAT FROM HER AMISH PAST

Eight years ago, a drifter destroyed Becca Miller's ties to her
Amish community—and murdered her family. Now a special
agent with Fort Rickman's criminal investigation department,
Becca knows her past has caught up with her, and doesn't want
to relive it. She's convinced that the killer, who supposedly
died years ago, is very much alive and after her. Special agent
Colby Voss agrees to help her investigate. Yet the closer
they get to the truth, the closer the killer gets to silencing
her permanently.

**MILITARY
INVESTIGATIONS**

THE AGENT'S SECRET PAST
by
DEBBY GIUSTI

*Available March 2014 wherever Love Inspired Suspense
books and ebooks are sold.*